HER BILLIONAIRE CHAUFFEUR

TAYLA ALEXANDRA

DEDICATION

Thank you to the One who gives His grace freely.

ALSO BY TAYLA ALEXANDRA

All Titles by Tayla Alexandra

Her Sweet Billionaire Romance Series
Her Billionaire Dream

Her Billionaire Jackpot

Her Billionaire Wish

Her Billionaire Chauffeur

Her Billionaire Scoundrel

To Trust Again - A novella

Finding Trust Series
Finding Alissa

Loving Josie

Reclaiming Bailey

Chasing Kennedy

A Billionaire's Tale Romance Series

The Billionaire Recluse

The Cinderella Ball

Bucket list Billionaire Multi-author Series

Beached with a Billionaire

* * *

GET TAYLA ALEXANDRA'S STARTER LIBRARY FOR FREE

Sign up for my no spam newsletter and get the novella – *To Trust Again,* the Christmas short *Wrapped in Love,* and *Brother of the Bride* (Companion to The Cowboy's Forbidden Bride) and lots more exclusive content, all for free.

Details can be found at the end of the book.

*L*ara Davies had never been more humiliated in her entire life. Sitting at the airport in El Paso, Texas, waiting for her flight back to Los Angeles, her body was numb. After a year and a half of chatting with him online, she'd finally agreed to meet him. Biggest mistake ever.

Dallas was his name. A Levi-fitting, Stetson-wearing cowboy who happened to live in El Paso. The lying creep.

They'd met once already, but she and Chloe had been so drunk that neither of them remembered. That weekend in Vegas had been the craziest, most mixed-up vacation ever. How was she to know that Long Island Iced Tea contained alcohol?

Let Dallas tell it, she and Chloe ended up dancing on the bar and flirting with strange cowboys from Texas. That wasn't something she would normally do, but as rumor would have it, that was exactly what she'd done. She and Chloe both. Although it had been embarrassing to come face to face with the man whose Stetson ended up in her hotel room, he'd made her feel at home right away. She'd thought he was a nice guy. He'd had that Southern down-home charm about him that made him seem honest and caring. He'd treated her so kindly and flattered her at every opportunity.

When she'd exchanged numbers with him on the plane trip back, she hadn't thought it would end in anything, but over the last year and a half of chatting with him via phone, video, and social media, she'd finally agreed to meet him. Biggest mistake number two. Right behind unknowingly ordering alcoholic drinks and meeting the jerk in the first place.

Now, as she waited for her flight back, she hoped never to lay eyes on another cowboy again. Not ever.

Her phone rang. Checking her screen, she saw her best friend Chloe smiling back at her. Relieved that it wasn't him begging her to come back, she answered. "Hey, Chloe."

"Where are you?"

"Airport. In El Paso."

"Are you okay? What happened?"

"Seriously, Chloe. I feel so stupid. How did I not know Dallas was married? We talked every night. On the phone, text, we even Face-timed! And three kids! I'm so embarrassed." She curled the top of the airline ticket in her hand.

"You want me to send Max out to hunt him down, lasso him up, and drag him all over town on the back of his horse?"

Despite her misery, Lara laughed. "If I thought Max knew how to lasso anything, or had a horse, I'd take him up on it. Max is more likely to hogtie himself and be dragged by the horse than anything else."

"Yeah, you're probably right. I'm so sorry, Weda."

Weda, the local Mexican street term for a white person, was usually used in a derogatory manner. Chloe, however, used it as an endearment for Lara, who grew up in Crenshaw, where the Latinos outnumbered the whites by more than two to one. Lara had learned to fit in and was soon taken in by her Hispanic peers. They'd given her the nickname, and she wore it with pride.

"I'm not. I feel sorrier for the guy's pregnant wife and children. She was livid when she found out he had a woman staying in their summer home. You should have seen her. I thought she was going to kick his butt all the way back to—"

"You didn't—"

"Didn't what?"

"You know. I mean, you said you wouldn't."

"Oh! No, of course not! I would never have an intimate relationship with—" She blushed. "Well, we did kiss." The thought alone that her lips had touched that of a married man made her wince. She would never have crossed that line if she'd known. She'd told him all of that and even refused to share anything more than a kiss until marriage. He'd even told her he had a spare bedroom. "You can lock the door at night," he'd said. "I just want to get to know you in person."

"I'm so stupid. How could I fall for that gentlemanly act? You met him. Did you think he was a scumbag trying to take advantage?" She thanked God she hadn't gotten the opportunity to spend one night with the womanizer.

"Well, I only met him that one time on the flight back, but he seemed nice enough to me."

"Right?" Before she could rip her ticket into pieces, she set it aside. She needed that ticket to get out of Dodge. "Good thing she rescued me before I became a victim!"

"How did she find out?"

"I don't even know. She showed up at his summer home, dragging her three kids behind her, dressed up like they were on their way to church. She was so pregnant, she was about to burst. I feel like such a home-wrecker."

"You didn't know. Don't blame yourself. You couldn't have known."

"He was so... ugh. I swear I have completely disavowed myself from men. All of them."

Chloe laughed.

"Don't laugh." Lara chuckled herself. "I'm serious. Even Chelsea can find a man. Why is it that I find all the jerks? I mean, first there was Thomas. He was an arrogant jerk who thought a woman should remain barefoot and pregnant. And then Boss..."

"Whatever happened between you and Boss? I thought you two liked each other."

"I thought so, too. We talked for a little bit. He took me out to dinner, gave me a polite kiss, and then — nothing. What am I, a leper?"

Chloe snorted. "You are not a leper, Lara. Don't worry. Mr. Right will come along. Give it time."

"Yeah. Says the girl who has it all. A handsome man, a baby on the way, a salon that..."

"Yeah, about that." Chloe grew quiet. "It's not doing so well. Max says I put more money into it than it makes. I'm thinking about selling. It was a bad idea."

"Nooooo... that was your dream. Our dream."

Although Lara was a part owner of the business, it was in name only. Chloe had fronted all the money for them to set up the salon in the middle of Crenshaw. It had been a way to give back to the community. The only problem was, they gave out more cuts for good grades and awarded more scholarships than the money they brought in. The venture was a serious drain on Chloe's dream and Max's pocket.

"I know, but if it doesn't start making money, I'll have to sell and give the money to the Guiding Hands Monkey Mates."

Lara busted out in an uncontrollable chortle, making several other patrons turn and stare. When the ticket agent looked up to see what all the racket was about, Lara covered her mouth.

Chloe always knew how to make her laugh. Even in the worst of times. The Guiding Hands Monkey Mates had been a charity her late father had threatened her with unless she found a husband. It was a charitable organization that loaned monkeys trained to assist the disabled with daily tasks.

A voice came over the loudspeaker with the announcement that the flight to Los Angeles was currently boarding. "Chloe, I gotta go. I'll see you in about two hours."

"I'll be at the airport to pick you up myself."

"Thanks, Chloe. I appreciate you being there for me."

"You got it, Weda. Get back here and think no more about that cowboy jerk."

Lara disconnected the call, gathered her carry-on bag, and stepped into the long line of passengers anxiously waiting to board the plane. She was all too happy to get out of Texas and put Dallas behind her.

A wife and three kids? Really? She shook her head. How could she have been so naïve?

After wading through dozens of people and finally finding her aisle seat in coach, Lara sat back and relaxed. *Two hours. Only two hours before I'm back home again.* And Dallas Parker would be a thing of the past. The image of his wife waddling up the drive, her belly about to pop, made its way back into her mind. She was so pretty. Beautiful, really. With her long blonde hair and curvy figure, she was a knock-out. And she'd cried. Right there in front of Lara, the woman had cried.

"Dall, how could you do this to me? To us?" Her three sweet children stared up at their daddy with broken hearts. "And in our summer home?"

Dallas had pleaded with and begged his wife for forgiveness as Lara stood outside, calling for a cab to take her away from the awful place.

"No more, Dallas Parker. This time we're through!" his wife shouted as the youngest child, not more than three, held his hands out and cried for his daddy.

This time? Lara hadn't remembered her saying those words when it had all happened. She was too worried about high-tailing it out of there. But the woman *had* said it. *This time... He'd cheated before.* Pressing her knees together, she rubbed her forearms. He'd brought her there for one reason and only one — to seduce her. She'd been so lucky to get out of there with her sanity, along with other things. *Thank You, God.*

Cringing at the thought, she closed her eyes. It was all so unbelievable. And she was more than unnerved. She was terrified of what could have happened. No more. No men. No relationships. She was all too happy to live a life of celibacy.

Chandler and Dena sat in the back seat, chatting about what fun it would be to go on their second honeymoon. Their toddler CJ, or Chandler Jr., sat in his car seat and babbled in a language only he understood.

"You ready to be my A-number one pilot?" Chandler called up to Boss.

"As ready as I can be. Who's your number two?"

Chandler chuckled. "It's all you, big boy. You up for it?"

Boss had flown a bit in the Navy and loved it, but until about a year ago he'd wanted nothing to do with the military, or flying. That had all been a part of the past he didn't want to think about. His time spent in the Navy was better left behind. But last year, upon request, Boss had gone back to flight school. He'd earned his pilot's license and was willing to take the less-demanding and higher-paying job for Chandler. He respected the man too much to turn him down. It had nothing to do with money. Boss was wealthy in his own right. Chandler had been a good friend to him, and he'd do just about anything for the guy.

"You sure you don't want to find someone with more experience?" Boss asked.

"I wouldn't trust anyone to pilot me but you," Chandler answered. "I'll hire a new driver. That'll free you up for your own ventures. I won't be flying but a couple of times a year."

It was the ideal situation, if only he could put away the past. And her. And everything flying meant. Putting it out of his mind, he pulled into the resort where Chandler had taken Dena the day they officially met. They'd all had a good laugh about Chandler taking the cleaning lady to an upscale business meeting. He'd never tell that he and Max had made a bet whether Dena could hang with Chandler the entire time or if she'd run out with her tail between her legs. She'd impressed them all, especially Chandler. He'd fallen in love with her.

"Okay, out you go. Have a good time, kids." Boss jumped out to grab their bags from the trunk.

Chandler came around and patted him on the back. "I got this, man. Thanks again. You don't know how much I appreciate you agreeing to pilot for me. It's a serious load off my mind."

The little guy came toddling up behind his father. Chandler picked up the boy and pulled him into his arms. "Now, you want to take this little guy off my hands so Dena and I can have a romantic honeymoon?"

Boss pinched CJ's cheek. "No can do, chief. Babies are not my forte. You should have called Chloe for that one."

Dena came up behind, and CJ held his arms out to his mother. "Traitor," Chandler chuckled as he handed the boy over.

"Chloe is due any day now," Dena said, cuddling her boy. "There's no way she can keep up with a toddler."

"Yeah. 'Bout ready to pop." Chandler made an exaggerated popping sound and waved his hands as if there was an explosion.

"You stop it!" Dena slapped him playfully. "I bet you talked about me when I was pregnant, too."

"Not you, dear." He leaned in to kiss her and CJ pushed his face away. "You were as purty as a doll." He tickled his son as he leaned in for another kiss. This time he succeeded.

"And so is she." Dena gave him a look.

"Yes, dear. So is she, but not as pretty as you."

Dena rolled her eyes. "Boss, what do you have planned for your two-week vacation?"

"Check in on the stores, a little fishing maybe, and some good old R and R."

Chandler cuffed him on the back. "Have fun, Boss. See ya in two weeks."

As Boss jumped back into the limo and pulled out of the parking lot, visions of taking his boat out on the lake ran through his head. He was due for a good long break, and he was going to take it.

His phone rang through the Bluetooth connection in the limo. On the screen scrolled a number. A number he'd never seen before. An unknown number. *Did Chandler forget his phone again?*

He pressed a button on the screen and connected the call. "Hello?"

"Hello. Is this Petty Officer First Class Callan Hemsworth?" a man's voice spoke across the limo's speakers.

"Uh, yeah. Who's this?" No one had addressed him as a petty officer in over fifteen years.

"Sir, this is Petty Officer Gonzales from NCTAMS Westpac. In, uh, Guam."

I know where NCTAMS Westpac is, you idiot. I was stationed there. Twice. "Okay?"

"Sir, I have a girl here. Her name is Kamia. She says you're a, well, she claims you're her father."

"I'm what? Hold on a second." Boss muted the call and pulled off the interstate. Just off the exit ramp, he pulled the car over into the nearest gas station. Removing the call from Bluetooth, he shut down the engine and put the phone to his ear.

"Okay. Come again?"

"This is Petty Officer Gonzales from NCTAMS—"

"I got that part. What is this about a daughter? What was her name?"

"Yes, sir. Her name is Kamia. Kamia Aguon. Unfortunately, her mother has passed away. I'm not sure of the details, but uh… well unless you are her father, Kamia has been orphaned. She says you're her father. She's provided her birth certificate to prove it. Also, sir, we have a record of a marriage between a Callan Hemsworth and Isa Aguon on file in your Naval records. Would that be you, sir?"

Boss stared out the window at an old man washing his front window with a gas station squeegee. *Isa is dead? I have a child?*

"Sir?"

"The girl. Kamia. How old is she?"

"She just turned fifteen."

The phone dropped from his hand, into his lap, and then down to the floorboard. Was Isa pregnant when he left? Why hadn't she told him?

"When can we expect you to be here? I'll need to notify the Command Master Chief of your arrival plans." The voice traveled from the floorboard all the way up to his ears. Why had he taken it off

Bluetooth? Hitting the steering wheel, Boss reached down and grabbed for his phone. It was a tight squeeze to get his oversized hands around his Android while scrunching his body between his legs and the steering wheel. He kicked at it, and it slid into his hand.

"Sir? Are you there? Hello? Sir?"

"Sorry, pal," Boss said, placing the phone back to his ear. "I dropped the phone. I'll be out there as soon as I can. First flight out. Is there somewhere I can call for details when I get there?"

"You can come straight here. Show your Navy ID at the gate, and that will get you on the base. Go straight to the NCTAMS building."

"Where is she staying? Is someone there to care for her?"

"Unfortunately, no. Kamia has no family."

"No family?" How could that be possible? Isa had a huge family. "Where will she stay until I get there?"

"Sir, we have found a temporary home for her here on base until you can come for her."

"Okay. Yeah. Let me make a few arrangements, and I'll get a flight out as soon as I can."

Boss disconnected the phone and dropped it into the center console. Staring into nothingness, he clenched his jaw tight. How could that be possible? Isa had broken his heart fifteen years prior. He'd never contacted her after he left. He just assumed she went back to her family. And now she was gone, and he had a child? Grabbing the phone again, he dialed Chandler.

"Eh, Boss. You just left us, didn't you? Change your mind about taking the baby?"

"Uh, no, Chief. Something big came up. I uh, I got some news." He wasn't sure if it was good or bad.

"Shoot."

"Uh, well, so I got a call just after dropping you off. I'm not sure ... okay man, I'll just come out and say it. I'm a father."

"A what? I didn't even know you were dating. Wait." In the background, Dena and CJ laughed and played. "Let me step outside for a minute."

The phone went silent for a moment.

"Okay, sorry, bro. Now when did you get this call?"

"About two minutes ago. Her name's Kamia. She's fifteen and orphaned on the island of Guam."

"Guam? Fifteen? You're messing with me, right?"

He wished he was. "No joke, man. I'm going to take a flight out there to meet her. I mean, I guess I'll be bringing her back with me. That is, if she's my daughter." Who was he kidding? The date matched up perfectly. Unless Isa was cheating on him, and he doubted she had, he was the girl's father. He needed no test to prove that.

"Guam? From your Navy days?"

"Yup."

"Tell me you didn't know. Was it just a onetime thing or something? I mean, I've heard about what sailors do when they get into port."

"Nope. I was stationed there for four years. A split tour. Married for one. The girl's birth coincides perfectly with the timeframe we were married. If Isa got pregnant while we were together, my daughter would be exactly Kamia's age. She's mine, dude. I just can't figure out why Isa wouldn't have contacted me. She had to have known I would take care of my daughter." Even if he hadn't been willing, and he would have, the Navy would have been sure to stick him with the bill. It made no sense. He'd loved Isa. The divorce had broken him in ways he could never have imagined.

"Hey man, handle your business. You wanna take the jet?"

"Nah, I couldn't do that. I'll take a commercial flight."

"I'd prefer if you did. I want you to feel comfortable by the time I get in with you." Chandler chuckled.

"You think I should? Really?" Chandler's new jet was a sweet ride. Fresh from the manufacturer and fully equipped.

"Yeah. Why not? It'll give the Bombardier a little work-out, and you can get familiar with it."

"Thanks, man. I appreciate it."

"Do your thing, Daddy."

"Ugh." A dad. How could I be a father? *I don't even know how to be a good husband.*

"Alright, man. I'll email you my flight schedule once I get it together. You mind if I take someone along with me?" He had no wish to make the trip alone. Besides the fifteen-hour flight, he wanted someone there to keep him sane while he met his fifteen-year-old daughter. His heart palpitated at the thought. *What does she look like? Her mother? Me?*

"Who you got in mind?"

"I do not know. Just not excited to go through this one alone. I'd prefer someone of the female persuasion. I have no idea how to handle a teenage girl."

"I know what you mean, dude. Yeah, sure. Get one of your... Do you even date?"

"Not really. I'll figure it out. Later."

"See ya, pal. Let me know if there's anything else I can do."

"Yeah. Sure." Like, take over fathership of a fifteen-year-old girl?

Boss disconnected the call. "Now what?"

He'd spent his time so consumed with staying away from life that he'd not made many friends. There was only one other person to call, and that was iffy at best.

Boss picked the phone back up.

2

*G*lad to be back home, Lara slid into the driver's seat of Chloe's vehicle. Chloe was as big as a house and due in less than a week, yet she carried it well. Her round face glowed with anticipation, and her eyes sparkled with life. Her sweet demeanor and loving disposition would make her an extraordinary mother.

"Thanks for driving us back. I'm so tired these days," Chloe said.

She leaned her seat back to make room for the extra added belly.

"Who knew being pregnant could be so taxing. You look like you need a nap," Lara said as she drove back to Chloe's house.

"I need more than a nap. I need to have this baby! She's killing me. Every time she moves, she bounces on my bladder. I almost peed on myself the other day."

Lara giggled. "Come on. I'll walk you inside, and then I gotta get back home to my solitary existence. Maybe I'll get a cat."

"Oh, please." Chloe laughed, but turned to her with a serious look. "You'll find him. Don't give up. What man wouldn't want all you have to offer? You are beautiful and kind and smart. Lara, you are so smart. Any man would be stupid to—"

"Yeah, yeah, I get it. Right now, I don't feel so smart. I feel like a complete—"

"Don't you dare go there. Dal—"

"Please don't mention that name. I don't want to think about that jerk ever again. I have stricken the name from my vocabulary."

Chloe smiled sadly. "You didn't know, honey." She brought Lara into a hug. "How could you have known?"

Emotions she'd held at bay since she'd gotten into that taxi in El Paso surfaced. Please don't cry. Not now. Once she got home, she planned to take a long bath, filled with water and tears. Mostly tears. A good cry always made things better. She took a deep breath as Chloe let her go. Saying a quick prayer, she asked God to forgive her ignorance. Remembering her mother's words gave her new confidence. "We are Christians, but that doesn't make us sinless. We make stupid mistakes, but God always forgives us." That, her mother had told her when she was fifteen and decided to go out drinking with her friends. She ended up with a huge hangover the next morning and harbored serious regrets. She had many regrets in her past. "We aren't perfect, honey. Just saved."

Chloe opened the door, and they walked into the house. Max sat on the couch with his feet on the coffee table. As soon as he saw Chloe, his feet immediately dropped to the carpet. "Hey, honey. It's Callen."

"Who?" Chloe asked.

"Boss," Lara whispered, remembering the day she and Max found out his actual name.

No one had known the guy's real name before then. At the mention of it, goosebumps raised on her arms. But he'd brushed her off like all the rest.

"Oh, hey, Boss," Chloe called loudly, as she flopped into the seat next to Max.

Max put an arm around her and spoke into the phone. "I don't know, dude. That's wild. A kid, huh?"

Lara waved to Chloe and headed for the door. She'd love to stay and listen to Max's conversation, but she currently needed to go home and wash Texas off her body. A state she would never visit again.

"Bye, Lara. Call me if you need to talk," Chloe called.

"Wait a minute. What about Lara?" Max said, making Lara stop in her tracks.

What about Lara? Lara turned, wondering if she should have moved her feet towards the door a little faster.

"I mean, if you need someone of the female persuasion, maybe Lara could go with you... dude, why not?"

Great, he was already rejecting her before she'd been invited. It was better that way. She didn't want to go anywhere with Boss *or* Callan, whatever his stupid name was.

"No, man. I mean it. Chloe is due any day, or I'd gladly send her, but Lara, she could—"

"Could what?" Chloe asked with interest.

Lara turned around and walked back into the room. "Could what?"

"Hold on, Cal." Max stuck his hand over the phone. "Callan has to go to Guam to pick up his daughter, and he wants someone to go with him. He's flying Chandler's jet. You up for it?"

Was I invited, because that did not sound like he wanted me to go with him? "I'm not really up for flying. You know I hate it. Besides, with Chloe ready to deliver any day now, I have to watch the shop." She did her best to bow out gracefully. Boss would thank her for it.

"I got that covered. Leanne can take over. Besides, business is slow."

Lara gave Chloe a why-are-you-doing-this-to-me look. Chloe smiled. "It'll be good for you. I hear Guam is a beautiful island."

Ugh. Even her best friend was plotting against her. She shook her head, vehemently.

"Aww, come on, Lara. He doesn't want to go by himself. He wants you to go."

I didn't hear him say that. "He wants me, or he wants someone?" She imagined the latter. And why should she oblige him after how he'd treated her?

"Here." Max held the phone out. "Talk to him."

Lara shook her head and pushed out her hand as if to ward off an evil spirit.

"Come on," Max whispered. "He's desperate."

Oh great. Thanks.

"Max! Don't say it like that." Chloe smacked playfully at her husband.

"Like what? Oh, I didn't mean it like that. I just meant that he needs someone to fly with him on short notice. That's all."

Lara's shoulders slumped as she begrudgingly took the phone. "Hello?"

"Oh, hi, Lara. How are you?" His deep, authoritative voice was always one that mesmerized her. Even now, it sent emotions whirling within her. Those piercing blue eyes that held her captive each time she'd ventured to look into them.

"I'm okay." Besides just finding out my phone boyfriend is married. "What's up?"

"It's a long story that I don't have time to go into detail with, but if you would accompany me on the trip, I can tell you all about it on the way."

Lara dropped her head. How could she say no to Callan Hemsworth? He was all muscly and handsome, and she wouldn't have admitted it out loud, but she'd been crushing on him ever since that day she first met him. That was why she went to meet "Texas jerk" in the first place. To take her mind off Boss's rejection.

"Yeah. Okay. When do we leave?" It was the personality flaw that got her in trouble on more than one occasion — the inability to say no. She regretted agreeing as soon as the words left her mouth.

"Tonight. I'll pick you up in about three hours. Pack a bag for about a week."

Tonight? "Wow. Okay. You want me to meet you somewhere?"

"I'll pick you up at your place. Same house on Ginger street, right?"

"Same house."

"Okay. See ya around seven?"

Lara looked at her watch. That was less than three hours away. "Yeah, okay."

She handed the phone back to Max and stared at Chloe. "What am I doing?"

"It'll be fun. Get your mind off Texas."

"Texas?" Max asked. "What happened in Texas?"

"Don't ask," Chloe and Lara said in unison.

"Right. Okay." Max put up a hand. "It wouldn't have anything to do with those guys you two danced on the bar top for in Vegas, would it?"

"Didn't I say don't ask?" Chloe pinched him under his forearm.

"Ouch!" Max pulled his arm away. "You sure are grumpy when you're as big as a balloon."

Chloe slapped him. "That's your daughter in there. Be nice."

"It is, isn't it." Max rubbed Chloe's belly. "Sorry about that, Little Maxine."

"We. Are. Not. Naming. Her. Maxine."

Lara laughed. "I better go get ready. Man, I hate flying." *I should have settled for buying a cat.* At least then she'd have an excuse not to spend an entire week with Callan Hemsworth. *Ugh!* Thankful she'd left her car at their house not wanting to spend the money on airport services, she pulled out her keys. "So, what's this all about, anyway?"

Max gave her what little detail he knew. Boss had a fifteen-year-old daughter on Guam. Claims he never knew about her. With what she knew about Boss, it sounded about right. He may have been a jerk to her, but she couldn't see him brushing off his responsibilities. Like it or not, Boss was a very put together guy.

With nothing more to say, and time running out, she left for her Kia. She would get that tear bath yet.

On the drive home, her phone rang. Hoping it was Boss calling to cancel, she lifted it from the center console and checked the call. It was her mother.

"Hey, Mom," she answered, trying to sound upbeat.

"Your father and I wanted to invite you over for dinner on Sunday after church. Can you make it?"

Immediately she thought of Boss. Maybe she could beg out saying she had a prior engagement. Yeah right, dinner with the parents. Not an acceptable excuse. "Sorry, Mom. I'm taking a flight out tonight. I'll be gone for a week."

"But, honey, you just got back. What's wrong with you? You hate flying."

Lara hadn't dared tell her mother she'd gone out to meet a man she didn't know quite as well as she'd thought she did. Instead, she had lied. She felt terrible about that, but what was done was done. There was no use explaining it all now.

"It's my friend. He has to make a trip to Guam and wants me to ride along with him." At least this time, she'd told the truth.

"Guam? Isn't that an island? What in the world is your friend going there for? And did I hear you say — him?"

"Yes, Mom. Purely platonic. He was stationed there in the Navy a long time ago. He just needs to wrap up some business and wanted me to ride along with him."

"I don't know, Lara. It sounds like a big trip. You'll be staying in separate rooms, right?"

"Yes, Mom. As I said, I'm just doing a favor for a friend." She pulled into the driveway of her apartment. "We'll only be gone a week. I'll come for dinner next Sunday."

Her mother sighed. "Okay, then. But be careful. I don't like the idea of you being alone with a man. Even if he is a friend. You know what happened to Jewel."

Jewel, her younger sister, was only a year her junior and had made every effort to drive her parents crazy. With one scheme after another, she'd landed herself in hot water more times than not. After spending five months in jail on a check fraud charge, she hadn't been seen since.

"Okay, Mom. I'll be careful." Her face heated. She was thirty-four. When would her mother trust her to make good decisions? Dallas, with that stupid grin and corny cowboy hat, popped into her head. Okay, maybe she hadn't always made the best choices. And maybe this one wasn't so good either. But she'd said she would go, so she would.

"I love you, sweetie."

"Love you too, Mom. Tell Dad to buy me a big juicy steak for next Sunday."

Her mother laughed, and Lara disconnected the call. Her father would buy the 75-25 ground beef on sale and a pack of hot dogs. But boy could he whip up some great burgers. Still, her father refused to divulge the spices he used to make them taste so mouthwatering good. "Family secret," was always his answer. "Only the men in the family get it. If you go on and get yourself hitched, I'll pass it down to your husband." *Fat chance of that.* But that didn't matter. She'd always be the favorite of her parents' five kids.

With three older brothers off doing their own thing, and her younger wayward sister running the streets defying every authority she could, Lara got most of the attention. Two of her brothers were married, the other off in the Navy. Then again, as soon as grandchildren came into the picture, she'd be chopped liver. The thought brought her back around to Boss and just how little she knew about him. He'd been a serviceman, married, and now has a kid. What else did she not know about the man?

Sighing, she parked the car in her designated parking space and slid out. Checking the time on her dash, she decided to get a move on. With only two hours to get ready or back out, she headed for her one-bedroom apartment. As nervous as she was, something told her she wouldn't miss an opportunity to spend a week with Callan Hemsworth, The Man of Mystery. Even if she spent it flying fifteen hours over the ocean. If nothing else, she smiled at the thought of paying him back for not calling her after their one and only date.

Boss rushed to get his flight plan ready and pack his bags all at once. All the while, the vision of a teenage Isa roamed around in his mind. Was she as feisty as the woman he'd left behind? Would Kamia hate him for deserting her? Where was the rest of Isa's family? So many questions, yet not a single answer for the taking. The angst and anger of it all frustrated him to no end. *Why?*

It would be almost a fifteen-hour flight with one stop for fuel in Hawaii. His thoughts turned to Lara. He liked the girl on the few times they spoke and that one date, but even after fifteen years, he couldn't seem to get over Isa and what she'd done to him. And now, anything with Lara was completely out the window. She was not his first choice of passengers on the trip, but he needed someone to go with him. Someone to keep him sane during the flight. To be there when he met his daughter. He knew absolutely zilch about teenage girls. He had no other choice. Lara was free to go, and like it or not; he needed her. But he would keep his distance. Play it cool. Meet his daughter and bring her back to the states. Dealing with a teenager would take the pressure off him to revisit why he'd dumped Lara in the first place.

Glancing around his room, he took it in. His condo was a bachelor pad. Nothing about it spoke family. What am I going to do? Where am I going to put her? Boss had money. Working for Chandler paid exceptionally well, and his investments had paid off considerably. Last time he checked, he was worth just over a billion. What chauffeur on the face of the planet could say they were worth more than him? Of course, chauffeuring for Chandler was a mere side job. His big money came from his line of fishing stores.

And still, he lived in a two-bedroom condo. The second bedroom, well, that was filled with products of his favorite hobby — building model airplanes. The old WWI bombers to be specific. Plexiglass cases decorated shelves all over the room with his latest builds. It was not a girl's room, for sure. There wasn't even a bed or a dresser for her. He'd have to rectify that, but for the moment he needed to finish packing and grab Lara. He threw a week's worth of clothes into his suitcase, tossed in the swiss army knife Chandler got him the prior Christmas, and looked over at his fishing pole sitting in the back of his closet. So much for that fishing trip he had planned. Briefly, he thought about taking one with him. Guam was excellent for fishing. The thought of fresh Mahi Mahi made his mouth water.

Would he have time for fishing? Probably not. He turned. Maybe another time. Looking around, he saw nothing left to pack. He closed his baggage, lifted it off the bed, and rolled it out.

Getting into his BMW Z4 convertible, he sighed. How would he get the three of them back in a two-seater car? With every moment of thought, more issues seemed to arise. The truth hit him like a cast iron cooking pan. He was not ready to be a father. Physically or mentally.

But as fate would have it, that was exactly what he would become in less than the three to four days it took to establish paternity. The Navy had their own ways of doing things. Their motto was — hurry up and wait. Which to him meant — get here quickly and then we will take three weeks to establish whether you are the father, another week to decide whether you are fit to take her, and then at least two more to release the girl into your custody. That was the old Navy. He hoped today's Navy was much quicker because he had a week, two tops.

Thirty minutes later, and ten minutes late, he pulled into Lara's apartment complex. Idling right in front of her window, he honked the horn. She peeked out and then opened the door. Jumping out of the car, he grabbed her luggage and squeezed it in next to his in the tiny trunk. Hoping he wouldn't need a bungee cord to close the thing, he pushed hard on the top.

"Hey, you're going to crush my snacks."

Snacks! Why hadn't he thought about that? It was almost a fifteen-hour flight. What did he plan to eat?

"Sorry about that." He didn't turn to her, just one look and he would dissolve like ice cream on a hot summer day. "You got enough in there for two or should I hit the 7 Eleven on the way?"

"I could share. If you are nice."

He looked at her. She was grinning from ear to ear. Her mesmerizing green eyes tried to suck him into their depths like a swirling drain. *Keep your cool, man. Keep your cool.* He looked away.

"I'm always nice."

He continued to push and pull on the luggage until he got it wedged in tight. He closed the trunk and headed to the driver's seat. Mumbling, she made her way to the passenger's seat.

"What was that?" he asked.

"I was only saying you used to be nice. Or at least I thought."

Oh, no. Here we go. We haven't even gotten on the plane yet. "Look, Lara. I apologize for not getting back to you. Things have been rough." He started the car and let it idle. "If you haven't noticed, I apparently have a teenage kid I never knew about."

Lara rolled her eyes. "One you just found out about yester — you know what, never mind. It's none of my business."

"If you don't want to go, tell me now. I don't have time to bring you all the way back here once we're on the road."

"I'm good." Lara turned her head straight forward and stared her gorgeous greens out the front window.

Boss sighed. "Fine."

He pulled out and headed to the small airport where Chandler kept his new Bombardier 6000 jet. He'd worry about making things right with Lara after they've boarded the plane and headed for Hawaii. Maybe he'd even offer to stay a day or two in Honolulu with the girls if they had time.

"Fine." She threw her hands over her chest.

By his best guess, she was the kind of girl who always had to have the last word. He grinned. It was going to be a fun trip.

3

hy, why, why?

As Lara climbed into the passenger seat of the monstrosity of an airplane she would spend the next fifteen hours in, she questioned her sanity. She absolutely hated flying. Commercial flights were bad enough that she had to take an aisle seat just so she couldn't see what was going on, and here she was staring out a huge picture window with the view of everything in sight. Take-off and landing were the absolute worst.

And to top it off, Boss acted like a grade-A jerk. Okay, so she had started it with her snarky comment, but after what she'd been through with — she refused to name that state. Not even in her mind. And then there was Boss himself. Callan Hemsworth, the man with a personality disorder. One moment he was Callan — the perfect gentleman, sweet and kind and the next he was Boss — All business, stuffy and impersonal. As he climbed into the driver's seat or what-ever they called it on an airplane, Lara thought, maybe he was one of those people who had several personalities and gave them each a name. A man version of Sybil. Maybe she would see some more of his fine personas. If she were lucky, she'd meet a little girl hiding deep inside his psyche. At that thought, she let a giggle slip. Boss stopped his fidgeting with the console buttons and glanced at her. Those eyes gleamed at her, making her forget for a moment just how mad she was at him.

"What's so funny?" he asked as he pulled his seatbelt on around him.

"Not a thing." She held back the need to smile.

"Good. We're all loaded up. Fasten your seatbelt."

His words broke the spell cast over her. Without a word, Lara complied. *Not even a please?* Maybe she'd see Callan before the flight was over. *Fat chance of that.*

Lara leaned her head back and closed her eyes as Boss prepared for take-off. When she felt a nudge, she opened them and looked his way.

"Here." He held out his hand, his eyes remaining on the tarmac. Inside contained a small square package that looked like one of those cleansing wipes you get after eating at a greasy BBQ joint.

When she didn't take it, he looked her way. "What's that?" *Do I have food on my face?* She hadn't eaten since she got back, so there was no chance of that.

"For motion sickness. Open it up and place it behind your ear."

"Oh." She took the offering. A glimpse of Callan had returned for a moment. "Thanks." But how did he know?

After fifteen more minutes of doing some kind of checks and balances and receiving the okay from the air traffic controller to proceed, Boss turned to her. "Ready for take-off?"

Too late to back out? "Ready as I'll ever be," she answered, leaned her head back, braced the arms of her chair and closed her eyes.

Boss chuckled. "Relax. It's not as bad as you think."

"Right," she answered, but did not loosen her grip or open her eyes. If she were going, she would do it her way. Eyes closed, holding her breath until the plane was safely in the air.

"Suit yourself."

The next thing she knew, her body thrust back, sucking her to the seat. She squeezed her eyes tighter. *Breathe, Lara, breathe.* Not possible. She was an expert at holding her breath during take-offs and landings. People told her she'd get over her fear the more she flew. They lied.

Once they were stable in the air, a million miles above the earth, Lara chanced to open her eyes. A dizzy feeling rushed over her at the sight. All around her was nothing but sky and clouds. The scene was surreal, beautiful, heavenly. If she could only escape the thought of being so high above the world in a metal contraption that could fall out of the sky at any moment, maybe she could enjoy it. Okay, so maybe she'd watched too many action movies. That stuff was rare in real life. Still, with her luck, she would be that rare instance where the plane would... *don't think about it.*

"Beautiful, isn't it?" Boss asked.

"Yeah, it is. I'd still rather be on the ground." Why couldn't she be nice?

Ignoring her remark, he said, "I grabbed us a bag lunch from the hangar store and some more snacks for the trip. I put them in the galley. There's a case of water, and some soda's in the fridge."

There's a fridge? A galley? *What else is back there?* "Thanks."

"If you don't feel comfortable up here next to me, feel free to take a seat in the back. This thing is made to carry up to seventeen passengers. There are plenty of seats. There's a bed back there, too. Small but looks comfortable."

She would rather go in the back, find that bed and cuddle up underneath whatever blanket was provided, and sleep until they landed, but something told her to stay put. "I'm good for now, thanks."

"Your choice."

Now, who is being snarky? It was going to be a long trip.

After an excruciatingly long hour of hearing nothing other than the hum of the airplane and a bit of chatter on the radio thingy, Lara reached down and grabbed a book from her bag. No sooner did she open it to her bookmarked page did he speak. *Go figure.*

"How's the salon business going?"

She closed her book and placed it on her lap. "Not so good. Chloe wants to sell. It was a great idea, but with the baby coming and the fact that we are giving away more cuts than we sell, our profit margin is, well, we aren't making any money from it."

"How do you feel about that?"

"Like my dream is getting flushed down a slow clogged drain."

"What you need to do is promote it more. Get more clientele over the age of eighteen. Maybe add one of those nail-doer people."

Nail-doer people? She held in a giggle. "Yeah. Being that we are in a lower-income part of town across from the local high school, we aren't getting the right business to keep us going."

"Nail-doers. I'm telling you. You need to make an entire section for nails. People love that stuff, and that would give you an extra edge."

"Yeah, thanks." Since when was he interested in the salon market?

"Ever thought of buying Chloe out?"

"If I had that kind of money, I would. In a heartbeat."

"Hm. You never know."

What was that all about? *Whatever.* Lara picked her book back up and opened it. She read about three lines before he spoke again. "Ever thought of hiring a marketing specialist?"

"A what?"

"You know, someone to help you advertise your business. It's a great cause, giving haircuts away for good grades. And scholarships on top of that. People like to hear when things are done to bring up a community. I bet you could get—"

"Wait — how do you know so much about this? Aren't you a chauffeur?" Ex-Navy?

"I have made some wise investments. Own a couple of shops. I can lend you my agent if you like."

Shops? What kind of shops? How much is this guy worth? "Yeah, uh, thanks for the advice. I'll talk to Chloe about it. She's pretty set on selling."

"Lemme know. I might be interested in buying."

Lara stared at him for a long moment. What was up with the guy? Why would he want to buy a salon? "I'll let you know."

And the mystery continued. Lara didn't know who the man was who sat next to her. Mind-blowing.

❧

Boss grinned at the girl snoring softly in the seat next to him. She was a tough one. He'd offered her to take the bed in the back, but she refused. Instead, she sat, her head hunched over in what looked like an extremely uncomfortable position, fast asleep.

What was it about the girl that made him want to give up the bachelor life? Whatever it was, had made him avoid her like the plague. And that was not an easy task with her being so close to Max and Chloe. Whatever function was going on, Lara was most likely there. He wasn't a party kind of guy anyway, so he usually begged out, but this girl, she drove him crazy. And like the idiot he was, he'd agreed to take her along on the trip. A week or more with the woman would be sure to tear his heart into even smaller pieces. After Isa, it was already a shredded mess. And now she was dead.

"Hey." He nudged the snoring princess.

Her head came up for a moment and then fell back down again in a continued soft snore.

He nudged her again. "Lara."

Her cute snore turned into a snort as she raised her head and looked up at him. Her eyes were like tiny slits behind a cover of her eyelids. She looked so cute with her makeup slightly smeared, and a small stream of drool slipping down her face. She wiped at her cheek and yawned.

"Hey," he said again. "We're about to land."

Lara rubbed her eyes. Stretching her arms and arching her back, she yawned again. "Hawaii?" She looked out the window, still rubbing her eyes.

"Guam."

"Guam?" Suddenly her eyes popped completely open. "What happened to Hawaii? I thought you needed to gas up—"

"You missed it. Slept right through it."

"No way! Why didn't you wake me? I always wanted to visit... the airport... uh, in Hawaii."

Boss chuckled. "An airport's an airport. How 'bout on the way back we take a couple hours to visit some sights in Honolulu? Ever been to the Arizona Memorial?"

"No. What's that?" She leaned forward, gazing out the window at the tropical surroundings below.

"The USS Arizona. Sank during the Japanese attacks on Pearl Harbor. To my recollection, it was the only Navy ship that was too damaged to repair, so they let it stay at the bottom of the harbor. Now, it serves as a reminder of all the sailors and marines who lost their lives that day."

"How do you know so much?"

"Navy. Twelve years. I've been all over the world."

"Oh, yeah. That's right." She rubbed a hand at the back of her neck, making a slight guilt creep over him after he'd let her sleep so long in that uncomfortable position.

Receiving the go-ahead to land, he made his descent into Guam International. She watched him as he maneuvered the plane to the ground. Out of the corner of his eye, he could see those green eyes staring at him with her mouth hung open. She was adorable.

"Just how old are you?"

He chuckled. "Joined the Navy at eighteen, spent twelve years in, been out for another fifteen, you do the math."

Her fingers came out as she counted the years. For a minute, Boss wondered if she'd have to take off her shoes. "Forty-five. Geesh, you're ancient."

"Thanks. Now I feel old." The airstrip was just ahead. Maybe he'd land a bit rough just for that comment.

"No, I mean, you don't look that old." She backpedaled. "You don't look much older than me."

"I'm older and wiser, sweetheart," he said as he made a perfect landing onto the tarmac.

Lara took up her terrified stance of eyes clamped tightly closed, with white knuckles grabbing the chair arm. He just hoped her neatly groomed nails weren't digging holes in Chandler's new leather seats. He couldn't help but chuckle.

"Don't worry. They won't pop out if you open them."

"I'm not taking any chances," she mumbled.

Landing smoothly and taxiing around to the hanger he'd rented for the week, Boss couldn't help but admire the woman's strength. She didn't have to come. Overcoming a fear of anything was a huge step. If someone asked him to step into a pit of snakes, poisonous or not, he'd gladly decline. To this girl, flying was her pit, and she'd done it, eyes closed or not, she'd done it. He was proud of her, but wouldn't dare voice it.

4

_C_allan, the gentleman, helped Lara down the steps of the airplane into the hangar bay where he'd parked the plane. The descent was much rougher than take off, and she wondered if maybe he'd done it on purpose. She'd have to learn to keep her derogatory comments about his age to herself. Forty-five was older than her, but not much. Eleven years. If nothing else, the man had more experience than all the other men she'd dated put together. He was a well-dressed, confident, dignified man who knew what he was doing.

"Okay, I'm a bit nervous," he said, blowing her entire theory out of the water with only five words.

"About meeting your daughter?" They'd come all this way, and not once had they spoken about what they were there for. Of course, she knew. Max had updated her on the details before she'd left his house.

"That and uh, well, let's just say, Isa's family didn't kin too well to me."

"I thought — Max said your daughter didn't have any family."

"Yeah. That has me puzzled more than anything. The Chamorro people are family oriented. The poorer communities live in mostly the southern parts of the island. Many families, Isa's included, have several generations living in their homes. Isa's family was huge. That was a big part of—"

"Håfa ådai, and welcome to the island." A short, tanned man wearing worn black shorts and a blue Hawaiian shirt made his way to where they were unloading their bags.

"Håfa ådai." Boss returned the greeting and held out a hand to the man. "Name's Cal, and this is my friend Lara. It's good to be back."

"Ah, good to have you." The man gripped his hand. "Bendision. Friends call me Ben. I take care of the hangars. Might beaut you got there."

"Thanks. Company plane."

"I'll be sure she gets a good looking after. For a bit extra, I can give her a wash."

"That'd be nice." Boss pulled out his wallet and handed the man a hundred-dollar bill. The man most likely made his living mainly on tips, and Boss liked the Islanders. They'd been kind to him.

"Thank you, sir." The man shoved the bill into his pocket. "I'll take good care of her."

Lara nodded at the man and smiled. Not having time to do homework on the Island, she wondered what their nationality was, specifically. Boss seemed to speak the language with his "Half-a-day" greeting. Of course he did. He'd married into their culture. She wanted to pick his brain about the entire story of his lost love, Isa, but she didn't dare. At least not yet.

"So, Ben. Could you point the way to the car rentals? We're going to be here for a while."

"You bet. Head right on down that way to the main entrance. There'll be a couple to choose from."

"Thanks, Man."

Boss led the way into the airport and Lara watched the crowds of people strolling by. There were so many different nationalities found there. From Americans dressed in their military uniforms to Japanese carrying huge cameras around their necks. And then there were the native islanders who wore the casual attire of shorts and t-shirts. The differences were vast, but all seemed to get along.

Friendly smiles graced the faces of most as they hurried off to their destinations.

It was nothing like LA, where people snubbed each other at the airport, not taking the time to be friendly. And in the city itself, every other day someone was getting shot up in a drive-by or robbed at gunpoint, especially in the rough part of town where she grew up. She couldn't imagine that kind of scene playing out here. Then again, how much drama can be had on an island as small as Guam?

With keys in hand, Boss led the way to their rental, a four-door Elantra. At least he had the sense to rent something with more room than that hotshot convertible he owned. How he would get all three of them home once back in LA was still a mystery to her. Hopping into the passenger seat, she figured by the time they got back to the states, they'd be so annoyed with each other that she'd call Chloe for a ride. Chloe! Lara fastened her seatbelt. Why hadn't she thought of that? Chloe was due to have the baby in a week. Even if she made it back in time to be there for the birth, Chloe would be in no condition to drive.

Why, why, why?

"Buckle up. Guamanian drivers are extremely aggressive."

"Really?" she grabbed her seatbelt. "What's the speed limit around here?"

"Believe it or not, it's only thirty-five on the main drag. But around here, that's just a suggestion." He put the car in reverse and backed out. "The roads have probably been repaved by now, but back when I was here, many of them were made with coral. Ever drive in a place where it rained almost every day, and the streets are made of a mixture of coral and oil?"

"Uh, that would be no."

"When the oil rises to the surface of the slippery coral, tires slide. You learn to keep a safe distance at all times and don't count on your brakes to stop you if you're too close. Learned that one the hard way." He pulled out of the lot and headed into traffic.

"It's beautiful!" The picturesque scene mesmerized Lara. Palm trees and high-rise apartment buildings made the island look like a paradise. And there was beach as far as the eye could see. "I imagine this is what Hawaii would look like."

"Guam is like Hawaii to many of the Asian cultures, specifically Japan. It's a closer trip with all the same amenities. Well, mostly. You should have seen it when I got here in '92. Typhoon Omar had just hit and trashed the place. By the time I got here, the water was down, electricity spotty, and the island was a mess. It took years to recover from that guy."

Her first thought was, why would anyone live on an island with such natural disasters and —

"A year later, an earthquake of 7.8 hit the island creating a Tsunami that caused over two hundred million dollars of damage."

"Nice place." And why are you telling me this? "Wait? That doesn't add up. I thought you said your daughter is fifteen."

"She can count," he said. His tone was teasing. Even so, it sounded as if he were mocking her intelligence. "Came back in 2002. Yep. Loved it so much, I came back for more."

Lara got the feeling there was more to it than that. Had he and Isa met in 1992, fell in love, and then he came back to be with her again? *Okay, your imagination is getting away with you.*

"Anyway. So, I'd like to offer you food first, before we see about my dau— uh Kamia, but I'm anxious to get this all over with. Think you can wait a couple of hours?"

"Sure. Do you think she's not your daughter?"

"Chances are, she is. I will know when I see her."

"Oh. Okay."

"If you haven't noticed, Chamorro's are dark-skinned. They are indigenous to the island. That means they are native to—"

"I know what indigenous means," Lara interrupted.

"Okay then. Anyway. A mix of Caucasian and Chamorro would create a light-skinned, mulatto type of look. If Isa was seeing someone else, it was not an American. That I am sure of. Anyway, her daughter would look completely —"

"Do you want her to be yours?"

Boss turned into a long line of cars waiting to enter a military installation. NCTAMS Westpac, the sign said. A man dressed in a white uniform with three chevrons on his sleeve stood outside a security station, his face stern. With each car that approached the gate, he held his hand out to stop them, then waved them through with a hand stretched out and then to his chest. His stern demeanor, unfailing. When they made it to the front, the man held his hand out and then ducked his head into the car.

"No sticker?"

Boss pulled his wallet out and handed him his military ID. "I'm here in an official capacity."

"Pull up into the registration office." The man pointed. "Bring your ID, registration, and insurance to the counter, and they will issue you a day pass."

"Thanks." Boss sighed and pulled into the parking lot of the building. "Be right back."

Fifteen minutes later he was back, a piece of paper in hand. He opened the door, shoved the document on the dash and started the engine. They got back in the long line of people waiting to get in, and another fifteen minutes later they were waved on base and heading to — wherever he was going. Apparently, he knew the place well.

Welcome to Naval Communications Area Master Station, Guam, the sign greeted them. Boss continued down a long road. Excitement rushed through her. She'd never been on an island before, let alone a military installation.

When they reached the massive, two-story building, they shuffled through the big double doors. Just inside was a long red carpet that spanned across the main area. To the right, on the wall, were framed pictures of military officers. The first one read *Commander, NCTAMS Westpac*. He was a clean-cut older man that could have easily resembled her father. Down the line were several other men, just as old and dressed in the same decorated uniforms.

The place was crawling with men and women in the same clean, crisp, white uniform as the guy at the gate. Most of their arms held patches with three small lightning bolts and the same chevrons underneath. Some had two chevrons, some three, and several of them contained no chevrons, only diagonal lines. She was sure there was a meaning to it all, but had no idea what it was.

Boss walked up to the counter. "Can I speak to the Command Master Chief?" he asked the guy who sat bent over his desktop, typing away.

He stood quickly. "Yes, sir. Let me get him on the phone. Your name?" The kid couldn't have been over twenty.

"Callan Hemsworth."

"Oh." His face lit up. "He's been waiting for you. No need to call, I'll bring you right back."

⚜

The old familiar NCTAMS Westpac. It had been a while, but the place still looked the same. Following the Petty Officer of the Watch back to the office of the Command Master Chief, Boss felt his knees go weak. Was he really here again? On the island he had come to love and hate, all at the same time? Just entering the base had stirred up so many memories in him.

"Master Chief?" the young kid said, leaning into the room. "Petty Officer Hemsworth has made it in."

"Oh," the voice boomed. "Just the man we were waiting for. Come on in."

Boss entered the room, and to his surprise, the man sitting behind the desk had a wide grin on his face. He stood. "Well, if it isn't good old' Hemmie. Loverboy, himself. Who'd a thought we'd meet again, and under these circumstances?" The old friend held a hand out to shake.

Boss took it, happy to see a friendly face. "Billy the Kid, a Command Master Chief. How'd you get that position? Last I knew you were a measly Chief."

"Yep. And you had just got busted down to First Class. How's it hang — oh, didn't see you there." He stopped as he spotted Lara. "Pleased to meet you."

"Command Master Chief, this is Lara. She's a —" He looked at

Lara, who was almost hiding behind him. "A friend of mine. She accompanied me on the flight."

"No need for formalities, Hemsworth. Call me Bill. You're not a sailor anymore."

"Right. Then call me Cal."

"Have a seat, you two. I hear you flew here on the company jet. Big baller you are now, huh?"

"Got my civilian pilot's license beginning of the year. My boss was happy to let me try out the new jet. Said I needed to break it in."

"Bet you regret switching rates, don't you? Almost had your Navy pilot license, and an officer position to boot."

It had been the biggest regret of his life when he got grounded and forced to change rates. That was what had landed him in the Radioman rate. With the program he was in, once he got his license, he'd have been immediately granted the rate of Chief Warrant Officer. But that wasn't to be, and going from airman to seaman had been an awkward change, but it was that or get out, and at that time, he wasn't ready for the real world. So, he'd switched rates, and although his new, less appealing rate was boring, he'd gained a vast knowledge of computers. He didn't know then just how much that training would come in handy.

"It's all good. I got my wings anyway." He'd held plenty of contempt for the Navy after the unfortunate mishap, but he was over that now.

"Well, good on ya. But, of course, you didn't come all the way to the island to rub it in my face that you are going places and I'm still stuck behind a desk."

"No, unfortunately not." The thought of why he was sitting in the office of The Command Master Chief on an island he vowed never to return to, gave him pause. He was here to meet his daughter. He shuffled his feet under the chair.

"Tell me you didn't know."

"No idea, Bill. I swear."

"I figured as much. Not like the Hemmie I know to go and leave a child without taking responsibility. I know things were crazy when you left and these island people, well they aren't — it doesn't matter. You're here now. Let's get down to business."

No matter your first name, in the Navy you were called by your last. And if you were unlucky enough to get a nickname, it stuck. Boss would be forever called by that corny name in the presence of his former peers. Hearing it made him a bit nostalgic.

"Where is she?"

"As soon as I heard the news, Tammie and I took her in for the interim. Hasn't spoken a word since she's been with us. Understandable with the loss of her mother and being shunned by her community."

"Shunned? Why?"

"Not quite sure. Best I can figure, after you left, Isa had been pushed away. I don't know what happened between the two of you, and I don't want to know, but whatever it was, got her in some deep trouble with her village. You know the Islanders and their superstitions; probably thought she would bring them bad luck with a half-white baby."

Half-white. Bill had confirmed his suspicion. Kamia was his. She had to be. Boss was not about to tell his old friend what happened between Isa and him. It didn't matter. She was gone, and Kamia was his. After a moment of Boss not answering, the guy spoke again.

"Anyway, so we'll do a blood test on you to see if the DNA matches and if it does, she's all yours. Would you like to meet her?"

"Yeah." Boss looked at Lara, who sat quietly beside him, staring at her hands. "Guess I better get this over with."

"Let me make a call." Bill picked up the landline on his desk, spoke for a few minutes and then hung up. "It's all done. Tammie will bring her by. We are staying out in South Fin, so it'll be about fifteen minutes, give or take. Would you two like some coffee? Got a fresh pot of mud brewing now. Thick and strong. It'll grow hair on your chest."

"Nah, I'm good." Boss looked at Lara.

"No thanks," she spoke for the first time since entering the building.

"Well, I'm going to have me one." Bill stood. "Haven't had my fill yet." On the desk next to his computer sat a white coffee mug. The inside was stained brown. "Gives it flavor." As if he was proud, he tipped the cup to show all his years of hard work.

Lara wrinkled her nose and went right back to staring at her hands. He hated that she felt so uncomfortable, but it couldn't be helped.

"You okay?" he whispered, nudging her arm.

She nodded, looking up at him. "Yeah, just tired, I guess."

How she could be tired after sleeping a good portion of the flight was beyond him. He'd been up for over twenty hours straight. But she was in a strange place, and with jetlag and the time difference on top of that, he'd give her some leeway. The difference in time alone was enough to throw anyone off balance. It was already early evening the next day.

When a tap sounded at the door, Boss looked up. As it opened, his heart beat the tune to the star-spangled banner. He wasn't ready to meet his daughter.

A woman about three inches shorter than him and a bit thick around the midsection entered the room. Behind her was a young, lighter version of Isa. His heart stopped cold at the sight of her. She was beautiful, and somehow, beyond all reason, her eyes were as blue as his own. She stood about five feet five inches and wore clothes much too big for her. Her long dark hair looked stringy and unbrushed. Where had they found her? Had she been wandering the streets of Merizo?

"Come on in, Kamia," the woman pulled at her arm gently. "He won't bite."

Fear plagued him at the sight of her. She was only fifteen, yet her blue eyes held the bite of an Alaskan winter. She'd only met him, and already, she hated him. And yet, after only one look, his heart soared with love and compassion for the girl.

"Kamia," Bill said. "This is Hem — uh Callan. He's a good man. And we think he's your father."

"I don't need a father."

"Now, Kamia, what's a pretty girl like you going to do on the streets of the island? You have no family."

Boss's heart was breaking little by little at the sight of his daughter. How could he ever make up for lost time? At that moment, Lara looked up and put her hand on his shaky one. A calming sensation rushed through him. She was the only woman since Isa who made him feel that way, and now, there was one other. His daughter.

In a nervous voice, he spoke. "Kamia, I'm sorry for your pain. If only I'd have known." Lara's hand squeezed his, giving him the courage to go on. "But, I'm here now, and I would like the chance to be your father." He needed no blood test. "I have a home, back in the states, and I would be happy to have you come there to live with me."

"Who's she?" Kamia said as her eyes bore into Lara's. "I don't need another mother. Mine is dead."

"She's just a friend." One he wished he'd had the heart to take to the next level. But now was not the time to pursue that route. "A good friend."

"And I would go back to the states with you? What state?"

"California. You will like it there, I'm sure."

"I want to stay here." Her words belied the excitement that filled her eyes. "It's my home."

"Now sweetie," Bill spoke. "If you had a home here, we wouldn't have had to call this man. He flew all the way here to meet you. And if the tests come back that he is your father, he will be your best chance at a good life. The streets are no place for a child."

She frowned at the man, not caring an ounce for his title of Master Chief. "Then you can move here," she said, turning to Boss.

What did he say to that? He hadn't loved Isa enough to stay and fight for her. He had a responsibility to the girl.

Before he could answer, Lara spoke. "Kamia, I know what it's like to grow up rough. I grew up in one of the toughest neighborhoods in California. I was given the opportunity by a kind friend to move out of that environment, to better myself, and I took it. This is an opportunity to better yourself. If I were you, I would take it."

His savior. He wanted to reach over and kiss the lovely woman sitting next to him. It was all true, Lara had come from one of the roughest neighborhoods around. How had he not known just how beneficial she would be?

"I don't know. Maybe you aren't even my father."

"If I am not," He went out on a limb for the memory of Isa. "I would be willing to adopt you. Kamia, I want to give you a better life. I loved your mother, and the biggest mistake of my life was leaving her."

Her eyes glistened with unshed tears. "Maybe."

That wasn't a confirmation she would go willingly, but it was something.

"Bill," he turned to the Command Master Chief. "Lara and I haven't eaten since we got here. Could we take Kamia out to lunch?" Forget the fact that he hadn't slept the entire night and his body was thoroughly fatigued. He wanted to get to know the girl. Gain her trust.

Bill looked at his wife. She shrugged. "There's no protocol for this type of situation, but seeing she's in my custody at the moment, I don't see the harm."

Kamia's shoulders fell as if she didn't want to be alone with him. "Tammie, maybe you could come along? If it would make Kamia feel better."

"I, uh, yeah. Sure."

"No. It's okay. I'll go."

Was that willingness he saw in her eyes or just curiosity? Either way, he'd take it.

"Good," The Master Chief answered. "Then it's settled. But first, let's get that bloodwork done."

"No way!" Kamia held up her hands. "You ain't sticking me again."

Boss turned to her. Again?

"The corpsman assured me they have all they need from you, Kamia." He turned to Boss. "We already got blood from her and did a series of exams to be sure she was healthy. She's as fit as a fiddle."

Kamia put her hands down and loosened the worried frown that had overtaken her face.

"Okay, then. Let's do it," Boss said.

"I'll get someone to escort you to medical. It should only take a couple of days to receive word back. Seeing your circumstances, we will put a rush on it."

Boss nodded as the Master Chief made a call to find someone to escort him to medical. Lara's hand was still placed firmly on his, and the warmth of it gave him a new appreciation for the woman.

"HC2 will be here shortly to take you all down. Kamia, you are welcome to wait in the office if you prefer."

"I'll go. As long as they keep those needles away from me."

Bill chuckled. "I'm with ya, girl. Can't stand those things."

Kamia gave the man a half smile and proceeded to the door. "Let's go then."

5

---

*T*hree days later, Boss, Lara, and Kamia stood back in front of the Command Master Chief. In front of him was an envelope that looked completely sealed. Did the man think he was Maury Povich waiting to give the final results? "You are not the father." *Okay, stop it. This is a serious matter.*

"Are you ready?" he asked Boss first.

"I am," Boss answered, and looked to Kamia.

She nodded.

For the three days they'd spent in a hotel, with separate rooms, they had picked the girl up each day, and she'd taken them around Guam to see the sights. Lara's favorite was Talofofo falls. Despite the daily power outages, something they called load-shedding, and the high humidity, Lara was glad she came. The scene switched from the modern military homes to high-rise condos in town. From there it progressed slowly to run-down homes of the down-trodden community that dwelled at the southern end of the island. All in all, the people were nice, and she enjoyed her stay, but she was more than ready to go back home.

The Command Master Chief held the envelope out to Boss. "Would you like to do the honors?" he asked

"No. You go ahead. I don't know what all that medical jargon means."

The man shrugged, opened the envelope, and read the paper silently. For a long time, he did not look up. Either he was deciphering the words or just wanted to leave them hanging. Either way, she could feel the tension rising from Boss. Placing her hand over his once again, he looked at her and smiled. It melted her heart every time she saw it.

The Command Master Chief stood and held out a hand. "Congratulations Hemsworth, you are the proud father of a fifteen-year-old girl."

Boss let out a deep breath, and then he smiled so big she thought his face might break. His arm went around Kamia, and he pulled her to him. "Looks like I'm your Daddy," he said. "Whaddya say we blow this popsicle stand?"

Kamia looked up at him, but her face was not filled with joy. Instead, her brows lowered with a look of fear. Urgency. A need to run. Lara couldn't imagine what it would be like to be in his shoes at that moment.

"I don't want to go." Kamia pulled away from her father. "I want to stay here."

"Now, Kamia," the Command Master Chief said sternly. "We talked about this last night. Under United States law, you are still a minor and with no other family to speak of, you are obligated to go with your father."

Lara didn't appreciate the harshness of the man's voice, but she understood it. Kamia had no choice, and everyone in the room knew that. But it scared her. Lara reached out to Kamia as her head lowered and a sob overtook her. She was like a lost little girl being pulled away from everything she knew. Pulling her into her arms as if she were her very own daughter, she hugged her.

Whispering gently in her ear, Lara spoke words of love. "It will be okay. Your father is a good man."

Kamia nodded and held onto Lara as if her life depended on it. And really, it did. Nothing on the island held any good for the girl.

She'd lived a poor existence, looked malnourished, and needed a good dose of love. Lara vowed to God and her own soul that she would be a part of this broken girl's life. She said a brief prayer for Kamia and let her go. "Ever ridden in an airplane?" she asked, grabbing a tissue from the box on the table and handing it to her.

Kamia took the offering, let out a nervous laugh and shook her head. Sniffling, she wiped her face on the sleeve of her t-shirt, leaving the tissue unused. "Can I drive?" she asked.

Boss's face reddened. "Not if we want to get back to California in one piece, but I can show you a thing or two about flying. Whaddya say?"

"I guess I don't have a choice."

Boss shook his head. "Hey, kid. It's not so bad. I'm not as bad a guy as people say I am."

"I'll be that judge," Kamia said and stood to leave.

"Hold on a minute," Bill said. "We've got some papers to sign, and Tammie is off to get your belongings before you go and skip town on us."

Kamia sat back down, and Lara took the seat next to her. She put an arm around the girl's shoulders and tried to calm her worries, while Boss finished up the paperwork.

Fifteen minutes later, Tammie came in with a stocked full, green, Navy issue, duffle bag. She handed it to Kamia and hugged the girl. "Maybe when your dad sets you up with a computer, you'll write to us?"

Kamia nodded. "Thank you." She took the green duffle bag. "What is all this?"

"Compliments of the US Navy," Bill said. "Pulled some strings and Tammie was able to go out and pick you up some necessities. Won't be needing it much with your new daddy though, but it'll hold you over until he can get you properly decked out in some new duds."

"Thank you." She gave the man another half-smile. "I appreciate it."

"Nothing doing. Didn't have to put in one red cent. Part of the relief fund. You can thank Uncle Sam for that."

Sure, the girl had no idea who Uncle Sam was or anything else the man was saying, Lara rubbed the girl's back. "You ready?"

Kamia nodded.

"There's nothing else to do?" Boss asked. "A hearing or something?"

"Nope. Cap said if the results come back affirmative, you were free to take her. He's already had a background check done on ya. You are more than qualified to take care of her. If you just sign right here, custody papers will be expedited and sent to your home."

Boss took the pen and shakily signed for permanent custody of his daughter.

"Here's a copy of her birth record. You'll have to get her set up with a social security number when you get back to California. You should have no trouble at all. With these documents and a bit of explanation, you'll have her set up in no time."

Boss took the paperwork and gave the man a wan smile. "Thanks, Bill. It was good seeing you again."

The Command Master Chief thanked Boss for coming and told him to keep in touch. "If I ever get out of this monkey suit, I'll look you up."

Boss chuckled. "I'll be sure to get my number unlisted."

Bill guffawed and slapped Boss on the back. "Good on ya, man. Good on ya."

Grudgingly, Kamia left with Boss and Lara. The tension was thick all the way back to the hangar where Boss had parked the plane. It was going to be a long trip back. Especially for Kamia. The girl was leaving everything she'd ever known for a father she'd never met, a country she'd not seen, and all in a terrifying flying metal box.

As they boarded the plane, refueled, and took to the sky, Boss's emotions were heavily mixed between awe and fear. Not only did he have his long-lost daughter on board, but the way he saw Lara interact with her was a blessing. His feelings for Lara grew with each passing moment, yet the intermingling emotions he felt each time he looked into the face of his daughter and saw Isa was slowly tearing him apart. Again, he wished he'd not have left. If only he knew what had happened after he did.

Kamia and Lara sat in the back of the plane as he guided it toward Hawaii. He was glad that they weren't up front with him. He had long hours ahead of him to rehash old memories, and he didn't need the distraction.

"You okay back there?" he called.

As he glanced back, he saw Kamia curled up on the bed. A ball of fear. Poor girl. It would be a long flight for her to an unknown world. Lara sat beside her, rubbing her back. She gave Boss a thumbs up and then turned back to Kamia. Nothing about the situation was easy.

"Galley is stocked with food. Feel free to make yourselves a sandwich," he called to them. "And me, too. Ham, extra mayo."

No answer. *So much for that.*

An hour into the flight, Boss noticed his fuel gauge hitting the upper part of empty. "What the —"

He wasn't due for refueling for a good long time. And there was nowhere to stop until he hit Hawaii. He slapped the panel, but the gauge did not move. Looking back out at the tail of the airplane, he noticed a small drizzle coming from the tank area. He looked back to the girls, who were now both sound asleep. Boss panicked. He was losing fuel. It was still five hours to Hawaii, and he only had maybe an hour or less of gas. With the quickness of the drain, there was no way he'd make it anywhere. Dipping down lower, he spotted an island way off in the distance.

"Girls!" he called.

No answer.

"Lara!" he called again.

Lara sat up in the bed.

"Get a life preserver on. And for Kamia, too. We are going to have to make an emergency landing."

"What! Where?"

"Get your vest on!" he yelled. "Now."

45

Lara woke Kamia. "Where are they?" she asked in a panic. "The life vests, where are they?"

He dipped the plane lower as the island came into view. There was no way he'd be able to land on it safely. There were too many trees. "Under the seats."

Kamia jumped up in a panic. "What's going on?"

"Get your vests on and come up to the front. Lara, bring me one."

"Are we going to crash?" Kamia asked as she put on her life vest.

The land was coming closer. It was now or never. "Up front, girls. Hurry. Lara, you got my vest?"

Lara and Kamia rushed to the front of the plane. "I'm scared," Kamia cried. "I don't want to die."

"Remain calm," Boss answered. He didn't want to be harsh, but it would take all the concentration he had to land the plane safely and keep the nose up. And the chances of landing it without crashing were slim to none. His best hope was to get the three of them out with no fatalities.

"Kamia, get on Lara's lap. Buckle yourselves in."

He was taking a chance by having them up front with him, but he couldn't risk the chance of them getting separated. Guilt ran through him for having Kamia aboard. *I should have let them fly commercial, while I flew the plane back alone.* Always trying to be the hotshot.

He slung his life preserver around him and prayed. He didn't have time for guilt, but still, it plagued him he hadn't called on God once since he was a child. *If you are there, I need You now!*

Flying as low as he could get, he saw a small clearing at the other edge of the island that if he was lucky he could touch down there, and then slide into the ocean.

"Now or never," he said. "Brace yourselves!"

The plane was now so low that it brushed the tops of the trees. The clearing came into view, and Boss dove lower, doing his best to keep the nose of the plane steady. Their only chance of survival was if the nose didn't hit first.

Kamia buried her head into Lara's chest as the sound of trees hit the outside of the jet. The left wing caught on a high tree, and he watched as it ripped away, jerking the plane to the side. The disengaged wing flew back at the plane and crashed into the back. Kamia let out a scream.

He fought to keep his eyes open as the wheels bounced roughly onto the island and then back up again. It would be near impossible to keep the plane intact. He'd already lost a wing that was tittering from side to side from the lack of balance.

Touching down, there was not enough cleared space to stop the plane before it reached the water. It couldn't be helped. Keeping the girls safe was all that mattered to him.

The plane slowed its pace but rumbled and tipped, still heading straight into the ocean. There was nothing he could do.

"Get that entry open!" he yelled as the nose of the plane hit the ocean, knocking him from his seat.

Lara jumped up, leaving Kamia to drop to the ground, and rushed for the door. If they didn't let the water in, they would die a slow death at the bottom of the sea.

"I can't get it!" Lara cried.

The pressure of the water was already holding it too tightly. Boss jumped up and ran to the door. "Kamia!" he yelled as he helped Lara get the door open.

Finally, it opened, and a rush of water flowed into the cabin.

"We gotta get out of here. Now!" Boss called as the space filled.

Kamia stood stock still near the cockpit. Terror overcame her face.

Water rushed in, leaving them with no room to move. Boss waded over to Kamia and grabbed her by her waist. Pulling her out of the death trap, he said, "Everyone, take a deep breath."

Kamia took in a deep breath, and Lara followed suit. The water was up to their necks.

"Out!" he yelled.

Without question, the three of them made their way into the frigid ocean. Boss held Kamia tight, making sure he didn't lose her. Now would not be a good time to ask if the girl could swim. Boss waved one hand through the water to quicken their pace to the top. He'd gone scuba diving plenty of times on Guam, but this wasn't fun and games, it was life or death.

As they reached the surface, Boss was still holding on to Kamia.

"Where's Lara?" he yelled through gasps of breath.

Kamia shook her head.

"She was right with us. Where is she?"

"I don't know." Kamia coughed, her face riddled with fear.

He waited for what seemed like hours in the frigid ocean water. Ducking his head back into the water to get a look, the salt burned his eyes. With the water still settling from the crash, there was no way to tell. A sinking feeling hit him. Why hadn't the three of them held onto each other? Had he chosen Kamia over Lara? He'd certainly not made a conscious effort of it. He'd never forgive himself if he let her die.

"Lara!" he called, knowing it was futile to call for her. If she was underwater, she couldn't hear him.

Within seconds, she surfaced. Only she was on her stomach. *Oh, God. No!*

He let go of Kamia and swam to Lara. *Please let her be okay.* Kamia floated safely in the water with her life preserver. But where was Lara's? She'd had it on before she gave him his own.

He grabbed Lara and held her upright. Doing a sort of cross between the Heimlich maneuver and CPR, Lara came to with a cough. Water rushed out her mouth in spurts as she hacked up half the sea. He thanked God. Even though it seemed like an eternity, she hadn't been under the water for long at all.

"Are you okay? Where's your vest?"

She couldn't get a word out between the liquid coughs and deep breaths. It was okay. She was alive, and they weren't far from land.

"Hold her other arm," Boss told Kamia. "You can swim, can't you?"

Kamia nodded.

"Good. Let's get her to safety."

Even being a good swimmer, by the time they made it back to land, Boss was completely drained. Kamia looked like a drowned rat, and Lara, as soon as they hit land, was able to walk, ever so slowly, up the sandy beach.

Kamia and Boss helped Lara to the far end where the plane wing had crashed down the tops of several trees. The wing, the only surviving member of the plane, sat at the edge of the trees.

He knelt beside her, relief and a feeling he couldn't explain washing over him like the wave of the ocean. Her lips held a tinge of blue. He offered a quick prayer that she wouldn't develop any complications. He would have preferred if they had access to a hospital. But in the middle of nowhere… Before he could think of it, he brushed strands of her hair from her face, then quickly withdrew his hand. "Let's put her head on a life vest." Removing his vest, he placed it gently under Lara's head. Kamia dropped down next to Lara and coughed. They'd all had way too much salt water for the day. But they were safe. *Thank you, God.*

Lara coughed up an "I'm okay." And tried to lift her head.

"Get some rest," Boss said. She needed warmth, but there was nothing to cover her with.

"Why don't you stay here with Lara and I'll try to find something to build a fire with?" Boss said.

Kamia stared down at the sand, unmoving.

"Kamia? Okay?"

Her head nodded, but she did not bring it up to look at him.

"Okay, then. I'll be right back."

Shaking his head, he rushed off into the unknown jungle to find some kindling. With his anxiety level at an all-time high, he needed time to recoup from the anxiety that consumed him. With another prayer of protection for Lara, he began stacking whatever wood he could find onto the ground below.

It had been a long time since he'd started a fire without matches. The Navy hadn't taught him that. He'd have to rely on the old episodes of Gilligan's Island he'd watched as a kid. What would it be like to live on a deserted island? He was sure enough about to find out.

A noise rushed through the brush, breaking twigs. Boss turned to see what it was. He only caught a glimpse before it got away. It was big and round. That was a good sign. At least there was some kind of habitation on the island. Who knew how long it would be before someone would find them?

Snapping off a dead branch from an equally dead tree, he broke it into smaller pieces and bundled it up in his arms. A cool breeze rolled through the trees, making him shiver. His wet clothes did nothing to stave off the cold. The island was tropical, but that didn't stop his body from trembling. He didn't exactly have a plan, but a fire was of first importance. They needed to dry off and warm up before sunset. Next — fresh water. They would die on the island without some source of hydration. Trudging back to where he left the girls, he worried for their lives. Not for his own, but for theirs. How would he be able to watch them slowly die? Without fresh water, that was exactly what they would do. He asked God for one more favor. *Please let us find fresh water.*

When he got back, Lara lay on her side. Her head nestled comfortably on the life preserver. He dropped his stack of sticks and the bigger branches he'd found.

"How's she doing?"

"She's okay," Kamia whispered. "She's cold."

He patted her on the shoulder and went to Lara. Either she'd moved her position by herself, or Kamia had moved her to her side. Either way, it was an excellent idea. He wanted no chance of Lara getting pneumonia. Checking her vital signs, he let her lay there a little while longer to allow her some rest. But she needed warmth. His first task was to build a fire. It was the only way to keep them warm.

Boss grabbed some bigger pieces of the firewood and placed it on the bottom of his makeshift fire pit. He placed kindling on top and then went to work trying to create a spark to ignite the wood. For fifteen minutes he tried. Once, he'd created a little smoke, but other than that, nothing.

After watching his struggle to get it started, Kamia came over, nudged him aside, and set to work lighting the fire. Within minutes she had the fire going and was feeding the kindling into it until it grew to a good size.

Alrighty then. He checked on Lara again. The rise and fall of her chest let him know she was breathing, but her body was still much too cold. With nothing to warm her with, he hoped the heat from the fire would do the trick. Taking off his t-shirt, leaving only his tank top underneath, he draped it over top of her for a bit more warmth. The heat of the island had already dried it. He tucked it in around her hoping to warm her at least a bit more.

He stood back and watched the flames lick the evening sky. In another hour, by his estimation, it would be fully night time. And if the rustling he'd heard in the wooded area was any indication, they might need shelter. The idea of wild boars, or boonie pigs as they called them on Guam, was something he'd much rather catch than get caught by.

As was his ritual, he made a firm plan in his head as to what he would need to accomplish before nightfall. Usually, his mental check-list did not include things so desperate as building a shelter or catching dinner. Be that as it may, he was set on keeping the three of them alive — even if it killed him.

First thing — a shelter of some sort. Boss stared at the plane wing. Maybe he could do something with that and some palm fronds from the trees he'd spotted. He looked over to Kamia, who had a large stick in her hand. She was whittling away at the tip with her fingernail to create a sharp point. That's when it hit him. He'd thrown his pocketknife into the pocket of his pants that morning when they set out for their hike to Talofofo falls. Standing, he reached in and let out a gasp when he found it wedged in the bottom of his pocket. Thank God for Velcro closures. He tossed it to Kamia.

"You know how to fish with that?"

She nodded.

"Well, I'll be. We got ourselves a plan. Get that to a fine point and see if you can drum us up some dinner and I'll get us together a shelter."

Boss used whatever materials he could find to make them a shelter. Every few minutes he stopped to check on Lara. With the initial expulsion of water, steady breathing, and warming body, he was sure she was going to be okay. Still, he checked on her often. Guilt plagued him for allowing this to happen. *God, please watch over her.*

The sun went down quicker than he thought, and the shelter was not finished. Kamia was back within fifteen minutes.

"It's too dark. I can fish in the morning," she said.

"I agree. I can't see much either. Let's get some sleep by the fire, and we can continue in the morning."

Kamia nodded and laid down next to Lara.

Boss cuddled up on the other side to warm her with his own body heat. Putting his arm around her, it was the best he could do. He just hoped whatever was out there in the jungle would stay out there until morning. No matter how tired he was, sleep was not something he could afford. He didn't feel good about allowing his daughter to go to bed hungry, but there was nothing he could do about that at the moment. They were all safe, and that was more than he had expected. Boss prayed for God to provide them with nourishment in the morning.

6

With a raging headache, Lara sat up and took in her surroundings. The sun was setting off to the west, and no one was around. How long had she been asleep? She sat up, and a coughing fit overtook her. The horrid memories flashed back to her. She'd heard the voice of God under that water and had been so sure she'd meet her maker in person, but apparently, He had other plans because there she was, covered with Boss's shirt, on the banks of an obviously deserted island. She hugged the shirt close to her and looked around. *Where is everyone?*

The crackling fire only feet away warmed her body. Tipping her head to release the water that clogged her ears and impaired her hearing, she heard a voice call to her.

"Back to the land of the living, I see."

She turned to Boss, who was behind her tying palm fronds to the side of the broken plane wing. The wider end of the wing sat leaning against a palm tree, while the rest of it was held up by a wall of rocks.

"What happened?" she asked

"You tell me." He made his way toward her.

"I don't know. Where's Kamia?"

"Fishing. Why didn't you come up with the rest of us? What happened to your vest?"

That memory was as clear as day. "I was on my way up, and the strap caught on something." The struggle played in her head. "It was part of the plane. I couldn't get it off. No matter how hard I pulled, it wouldn't come loose. I was running out of air, so I unlatched my vest. After that, all I remember was floating to the top and seeing the sky break through the water. Then everything went blank." She didn't dare tell him that God had spoken to her, comforted her just before she passed out. That was her story alone.

"I thought you were right there with us." He sat down next to her. "I was so worried you had... I'm glad you're okay."

"I thought so, too. There's nothing like the feeling of all your air running out. It was strangely — not scary. I mean, once I got through the final freak out, it was like I went from consciousness to... nothing."

"You blacked out."

"Yeah, I guess so," she said. "I mean, I was right there, I could see the sun break through the top, and then everything went blank."

She tried to stand, but her head pounded so hard she fell back to the ground. "Maybe I better sit here for a while."

"Take your time. You need to rest your body, or we will have much bigger problems."

She hadn't been under the water for very long. She'd held her breath almost completely to the top. Just as the sun broke through, she'd lost consciousness. Then why did she feel so weak?

Boss got up. "I've got us a shelter going and Kamia — oh there she is."

Kamia came walking up the beach, her legs soaking wet, her lips held a tint of blue. Holding a bulge of something in the bottom of her t-shirt, she stopped in front of them and opened her shirt. Four barely alive fish flopped out.

"Nice!" Boss said. "We'll eat good tonight."

Kamia beamed with pride.

Boss turned back to Lara. "I worried about you for a while there."

"I'll be okay. Really. I don't think I took in that much water."

Lara watched as Kamia sat next to her and began scaling the fish.

"Get warmed up a bit, and then I need your help," Boss said to Kamia.

Kamia nodded.

"I can do this," Lara said, taking the knife from her. She felt horrible, but if she was going to help, she wanted to do the easiest task available.

"Are you sure?" Kamia lowered her eyebrows. "You almost drowned yesterday, you know."

"How long have I been asleep?"

"About twenty-four hours. You woke up a couple of times, then went right back to sleep. You don't remember talking to us?"

The thought that she'd got up and talked to them disturbed her. What had she said? "Don't remember a thing."

"You were so groggy, couldn't understand a word you said," Kamia answered.

Happy she hadn't professed her undying love for Boss, Lara nodded and grabbed a fish. Slowly, she scaled it. It was a good thing her father was a big fisherman. As a young child, she hated anything to do with the flopping fish or slimy bait, but as her older brothers went off to college or the military, it became something she and her father shared. Camping and fishing. Just her and her father. Only her dad always packed a rack to put over the fire. She didn't know how they would cook them without something to set them on, but she did as she was told.

"Kamia, come here for a second," Boss called.

Kamia huffed and stood. Lara turned her head and followed Kamia's pace. Knife in hand, she wasn't paying attention to what it was cutting into.

Turning further, a stabbing pain rushed through her thumb.

"Ouch!" Dropping the knife onto the sand, she grabbed her thumb. Blood gushed out. She wrapped the bottom of her shirt around it quickly and held her breath as she waited for the pain to subside.

"You okay over there?" Boss raised his brows.

"Yep." She pretended her thumb was not throbbing in pain.

"Kamia, help me shake this tree. There are coconuts up there."

Kamia looked up the length of the tree and then pulled at Boss's belt.

"Hey, what are you doing?"

"Give it here."

Reluctantly, the man pulled his belt from his waist and handed it to Kamia. By this time, Lara watched Kamia in fascination. She hardly had the chance to concentrate on the throbbing of her wounded appendage. Kamia stood on her toes and wrapped the belt around the tree. Kicking off her sandals, she hopped onto the tree, and like a monkey, she shimmied her way to the top. Boss stared in awe. He turned to Lara.

"Is she crazy or what?"

Lara laughed, still putting pressure on her wound as she tried to hide the pain. "She's something else."

Once at the top, Kamia dropped two coconuts yelling, "Look out below."

Boss caught one, but the other fell to the ground and rolled down the beach.

"One more, Kamia, then let's save the rest for later."

Another coconut came flying down at Boss, almost hitting him in the face. Lara laughed so hard she ended up in another coughing fit.

"You trying to kill me?"

"Guess she's not too happy with your piloting skills right about now," Lara said with another cough. More water came up, and she spat it out.

"Guess not. I'm not thrilled with it myself."

Kamia slid back down the tree and landed on her feet.

"Where'd you learn that?" he asked.

"Coconut milk will sustain us until we find water," she said and walked away from him.

Yep, she's mad. Lara couldn't help but find the humor in all of it. God had told her under that water that she would survive. She hoped that meant she would get off the island as well.

Kamia came back and sat down next to her by the fire. She held three sticks in one hand and a coconut in the other. Banging the spear she'd made into the coconut with a good-sized rock, she created a hole in it and handed it to Lara. "Drink. You will feel better."

As Lara drank the sweet liquid, Kamia took the fish and finished scaling them. Lara watched in awe as the girl cut off the head and the tail and then skewered them through the center. Placing more kindling on the fire, the girl placed the fish-kabobs at the edge and watched them smoke.

"Eat the meat. It's good for you." Kamia nodded to the coconut. "I can break it open for you."

"Thank you, Kamia. We'd probably die without you."

"You would not be here without me." Kamia's eyes never left the fish smoking at the side of the fire. With a quickness, she turned the fish over and stood. "We will need something to set them on once they finish cooking."

Kamia grabbed the knife and set off for the woods. Boss stopped what he was doing and called to her. "Where are you going now?"

She ignored him and kept walking.

"Where's she going?" he asked Lara. "I don't think it's safe in there."

"I'm sure she has more experience with it than either of us."

Boss looked out into the densely wooded area. "I better go after her."

"Maybe you should stay. She's dealing with a lot right now."

Boss came and sat down next to Lara.

"What do you mean?"

"She thinks it's her fault we're here."

"Well, that's stupid. It's not her fault. We lost fuel. There was no other—"

"Yeah, but if you hadn't come for her, the plane would have never gone down. She feels responsible. Go easy on her."

"That's — She couldn't — Wow. Okay. Yeah, I could see how she could feel to blame. But she's not. I chose to come here. I had no intention of getting us stranded." Boss picked up a twig and made swirlies into the sand. "What a mess I got us into."

Lara put her hand on his to stop the motion. "It's not your fault." A rush ran through her at the warmth he provided. "Let's just try to get through this and make it home."

"Yeah," he answered. "I better get that shelter finished."

As he was leaving, Kamia came back with several nice sized leaves. She pulled the fish from the smoldering wood and set them down on the leaves. One on each.

"These leaves are not poison. It's the best I could find." She handed a leaf filled with fish to Lara.

"Thank you, Kamia."

"Let me see your hand." Kamia pointed to Lara's hand, still wrapped in her shirt.

Lara pulled it away. Looking at the small chunk of meat she'd chopped from her finger, she felt faint.

Kamia produced a plant from her back pocket and snapped it in half. She rubbed it onto Lara's finger and then with the knife she cut off the bottom portion of her shirt.

"Kam — wait!" It was too late. The girl pulled the fabric away and began wrapping it tightly around Lara's finger. It throbbed as she continued to bandage, but Lara refused to complain.

"That will heal just fine. Let's eat."

"Should we call your father to eat?"

"Nope," she answered. "He can eat it cold."

"I heard that!" Boss called as he walked up. "You better stop being mean to your pops or I'll have to paddle you."

"You would not catch me." A small grin formed on her face.

They were going to be okay. If they could get off the island, they would be fine.

"I set up the best shelter I could make out of what we have. If we move the fire closer to us at night, maybe we can stave off any wild animals who might want to eat us for dinner."

"Stop it!" Lara cried. "You're scaring me."

"Boonie pig," Kamia answered. "We should set up a trap."

"I thought that might be what I heard," Boss answered. "But we don't have anything to make a trap."

"I can," Kamia answered before taking a bite of her fish. "Watch out for the bones, they are small and sharp." She nodded to the fish in Lara's hand. Still, she did not look at Boss.

"Thanks. I'll be careful."

"How can you make a trap?" Boss pressed.

"Easy. I'll show you."

"Yeah," Boss said. "I just need a few minutes of rest."

He hadn't slept the entire night. Lara could tell by the red of his eyes. Did he stay up protecting her?

"Yeah. Go ahead. You need some sleep."

Boss looked hesitant. "Maybe. But I have to get that shelter finished, first."

"How about you sleep until midnight? I'm sure we will be okay one more night. You look exhausted."

"Ten."

"Eleven."

"How will you know the time?" Kamia broke into their debate.

"Oh, yeah right," Lara remembered her cell phone that was sunk along with her purse at the bottom of the ocean. "Okay. Well, at least a couple of hours. I'll wake you once you have gotten at least a couple good hours of sleep."

"I will stand guard." Kamia took a bite of her fish and spat out a small bone. "I am wiser to the jungle than you two are."

"She's got a point," Lara said.

"No!" Boss insisted. "You may be wise to island life, but you are not strong enough to wrestle a wild boar."

"You!" Kamia pointed at Boss. "You are a — a — ugh!" She stood and made her way back into the wooded area.

"Kamia, come back," Boss called.

"Let her go. It's daylight. Lighten up. She's been a great help, and she's your daughter."

"Exactly!" Boss's voice raised. "I have to protect her. For fifteen years of her life I have not been there, I'll be — I can't let harm come to her now." Boss sighed and swiped at his brow. "I have to protect her."

"Looks to me like she can protect herself."

"Wait, what does that mean? My daughter?"

"Stubborn. She's bull-headed just like you, only she's young."

Boss rolled his eyes. "She's just a kid." Still, he didn't go after her. "How are you feeling?" He took a leaf wrapped fish from the ground and pulled off a piece and shoved it into his mouth.

"I'm okay. I think I got it all out."

"Are you tired? Maybe you should get some rest."

What was this new concern for her? Granted, she did just almost drown. "I slept the entire night while you stayed up, remember? I'm fine."

A loud scream came from somewhere in the woods and Boss jumped to his feet. "I told you!" he yelled. "What did I tell you?"

Riddled with fear, Boss's body took control of the situation. His brain thought of nothing but his daughter being attacked by a wild boar. As he ran into the woods, he called out to her. "Kamia! Where are you?"

It was already close to nighttime, and the woods were dark and dense. Lara was right on his heels. How would he live with himself if he allowed his daughter to be hurt only hours after taking custody of her? Who knew what kind of wildlife lived on the island? Chances were, not a creature on the place had laid eyes on a human being in years. Maybe never.

"Kamia!" Lara called.

"Over here." The answer came from not too far off.

Boss and Lara ran toward her voice. Neither of them could see much more than the trees directly in front of them.

"Kamia!" he called again. "Call out to us."

"Over here." Another scream came, only this time it sounded more like a squeal.

A boar. It had to be. Did he have her cornered? All kinds of scenarios ran through his head, and none of them were good.

"I'm coming!" Boss yelled. "Stay where you are."

He reached into his pocket for his only defense, but his knife was not there. In an instant, he remembered Lara had borrowed it to scale fish. It was probably still sitting by the fire. Great use it was to them there.

"There. Up ahead." Lara said. "I see her."

"Where?"

Lara ran ahead.

"Lara, wait. It could be—"

It was too late. She was off and running. How she had gained so much strength only twenty-four hours after nearly drowning was beyond him. Boss picked up speed to make it there before Lara did. He passed her up, and before he could stop, he toppled over something big and round. A squeal echoed through the woods, and he wasn't sure if it came from him or the lump he'd fallen over. Face down in a pile of debris, he listened. The squeal came again, only this time it sounded like the last breath of a dying animal. Sitting up, he saw Kamia. She stood tall over a dying boar.

"I got em!" she announced. "We can eat for days on this one."

Boss stood and looked down as the boonie pig took its last breath. His knife was buried deep in the pig's neck. Not knowing if he was more angry or pleased by her catch, he stared at Kamia. For a moment, words failed him.

"Are you out of your... you killed a wild boar?"

"Way to go!" Lara said.

"Are you okay?" Boss slowed his breathing and wiped off his pants. "You could have been killed."

"I'm doing better than you," she chided as he wiped the leaves from his pants. "At least I didn't end up on the ground."

"I thought it was you. That you were hurt."

"I've done it before. It's nothing." Kamia pulled the knife from the pig. Picking up a leaf, she wiped it off, closed it and shoved it in her pocket. "Grab a leg, help me drag this beast back to camp."

As if she had not done the most dangerous thing imaginable,

Kamia reached down and shoved a leaf in the wound. "That should stop some of the blood. We want to leave as little a trail as possible."

Boss stared in utter shock.

"What? We can eat for days off him before he spoils."

Boss grabbed the boar, lifted it over his neck and headed back to camp. "Hope you know how to gut one of these, because I sure don't."

Lara laughed. "Great job, Kamia. But maybe from now on, let your father do the killing."

Boss smiled. The girl was something else. Tough. He imagined she'd had to kill many a boar and learn to fish before she was old enough to read and write. That thought made him sad. She shouldn't have had to grow up killing animals to survive. Had she even gone to school? Did she *know* how to read and write? The island was not known for their higher education to begin with. Kamia was street smart. She knew how to survive, but would that be beneficial in her new life in California? There weren't many wild boars running the streets of LA. Muggers, yes. He'd love to see someone try to steal something from this girl.

"Why do you call him Boss?" Kamia asked as she and Lara followed behind.

"I don't actually know. Just a nickname, I guess."

"My mom called me Kammie."

Boss smiled. If only he'd had the chance to see her growing up. He'd have to put that in the past, though. It was what it was, and there was no use worrying about what he couldn't change. Her future. That was what was important.

"I like that." Lara tried the name out. "Kammie. My name is too short for a nickname."

"I could give you one," Kamia said.

"What would it be?"

"Mames," she answered. "In Chamorro, it means one who is sweet."

"I like it. Thank you. What does your name mean?"

"She is like a flower. Hate that name. I am no flower."

"I love it. It's a beautiful name."

"What about me?" Boss called back. The boar weighed heavily on his shoulders.

"You?" Kamia said. "Chatongo."

"What does that mean? One who carries boar?" Boss chuckled at his own joke.

"It means one who knows nothing."

Lara burst out into hysterical laughter. "Kamia, you are too much."

"Yeah." Boss hefted the boar up higher. He was sure there would be blood all over his clothes. "Real funny."

He played it off as if he was hurt, but he enjoyed the banter. It was much better than her ignoring him.

Once they reached the clearing, Boss dropped the boar onto the ground and went to work massaging his shoulders. "That thing is heavy. It can wait until morning to cut open."

"No," Kamia insisted. "It must be done now. If other animals smell its flesh, they will surely come."

Boss sighed. She had a point. "Okay, then. Let's gut this puppy."

"Bring him by the fire."

She sure was a bossy one. Boss grabbed the hind legs of the boar and dragged it to the fire. "Good enough, flower girl?"

"Good enough," she agreed. "Now if you can wash that blood from your clothes, I will gut the pig and roast the meat."

"Right now?"

"You think wild animals can't smell blood?"

"On it."

"Mames can brush the blood away that you dripped into the clearing." She looked at Lara.

"On it," she repeated Boss's words, grabbed a palm frond, and began covering up the blood. "It's almost full dark. You better get that fire a bit higher for light to see by," Lara said.

"On it," Kamia said.

The words sounded funny coming from the girl, but Boss had taken a swift liking to her tough attitude. He had no worries she could hold her own once they made it off the island. Boss headed out to the ocean to drown himself in sea water. The temperature was cooling, and he'd near freeze to death before he finished.

Heading toward the shore, a shadow of something glimmered off the small bit of light left. Something had washed up. He ran to it, hoping it was what he thought it was.

It was his suitcase. Boss dragged the case the rest of the way to shore. The day was already looking up. Placing the suitcase further up on the bank, Boss waded in the water and cleaned the blood from his clothes.

A wind rose up sending chills down his spine. The thought of sharks or stingrays in the water made him finish up quickly. Most likely they didn't swim that close to the shore, but Boss was taking no chances. Once he was good and drenched, he waded back out and grabbed his suitcase. When he'd purchased it, the tag had said water-proof. If that were true, he would soon find out.

Back at the camp, Kamia was teaching Lara how to gut the pig. He couldn't see but a silhouette of them but was sure the look on Lara's face was one of distaste. *Take that, Mames.* He chuckled. The name fit her perfectly. She was sweet in every way.

"Guess what I found?" he said as he walked up.

"A shark?" Kamia asked.

"Nope. Guess again."

As he came closer to the fire, he could see them both clearly. The way the red and yellow flames highlighted Lara's face was mesmerizing. She was stunning. His heart went weak at the sight.

"Your luggage?" Lara said. "Boss, that's great!"

"Maybe by tomorrow we'll get some more goodies washed ashore," he answered as he sat by the fire to warm himself. "They didn't tell me the thing doubled as a floatation device."

Opening his suitcase, he found that all his belongings were completely dry. Guess he didn't have grounds for a lawsuit after all. He chuckled at the thought.

"What's so funny?" Lara asked, her hands bloody from the pig they'd laid out on a bed of palm fronds. Spots of blood tainted the pink souvenir shirt she'd purchased on Guam. "Nothing. Mind looking the other way, I'm going to change my clothes."

Her face reddened in the light of the fire.

"Could you do that somewhere else?"

"Eww, yes!" Kamia said.

"Just concentrate on your pig, and you will have no chance of seeing my six-pack."

"Right." Lara turned back to the pig.

He was unnerved to venture too far away from the fire. It was full night, and he did not want to run into that dead boar's angry family member. He quickly pulled off his shirt and laid it close to the fire to dry, then slipped on another tee. Lucky for him, he hadn't packed any formal wear. He'd had no need for suits on the island. Pulling down his pants quickly, he slipped on a fresh pair of underwear and a clean pair of jeans. After, he set the wet ones next to his shirt.

"When you guys finish up there, grab something clean to change into. Tomorrow's a big day. We have to search for fresh water."

"Is it safe to look?" Lara asked.

"As if you didn't peek."

"Ugh," she cried and went back to work.

Kamia giggled and then spoke. "The meat will spoil by morning if we do not keep it cold. We can use that case to store it in the ocean water. First thing in the morning we can dry it into jerky."

"My suitcase?" Boss cringed at the thought of dead boar meat stinking up his expensive luggage.

"The seawater will preserve it a bit, but without refrigeration, it won't last until morning unless we preserve it properly. And as you can see, there is no daylight left for drying. Nana told me, never let food go to waste. We have been blessed with this meat, and we shall use every bit we can."

"She's right, Boss. You can buy a new suitcase when we get back to civilization."

"Right." He sighed. "I guess, if it means we eat tomorrow, you can use my luggage." He didn't care. He enjoyed the playful jibes.

"Fill it with salt water. The salt will cure it, and the cold ocean water will keep it from spoiling," Kamia commanded. "And maybe some of that wire stuff from the wing, you could tie it to a nearby tree? You must get it deep into the ocean where it's cold. The lukewarm water of the beach will only create bacteria."

"Have you done this before?" he asked. "You know, trying to preserve meat in a suitcase in the ocean?"

She stared at him, her blue eyes narrowed in his direction.

"Okay, okay. Fine." Boss chuckled and shook his head. Isa had raised quite a kid.

7

*W*ith Kamia fast asleep next to the fire and a portion of the pig roasting away, Lara and Boss spoke softly.

"How are we going to get off here?" she asked, concern shrouding her face.

"The plane was equipped with a black box. Once it hit the water, the locator beacon should have emitted a pulse. The battery can last up to thirty days. Chandler will alert search teams when he realizes we're not back. He's going to be plenty upset that his new Bombardier is now submerged in water, but they'll find us."

The look of worry on his face set Lara to questioning his theory. "You don't think they'll find us?"

"Oh, they will. I mean, I can think of only one instance that — not to worry, they'll find us."

"Tell me."

"In one instance, it took two years to find an Air France flight once it crashed, but that crashed in the middle of the ocean. The box most likely sunk deep into the water. Our plane crashed just offshore."

"Two years? Are you serious?" Lara's mind whirled with crazy scenarios. Could they possibly survive on an island for two years or more?

"They'll find us."

"But what if—"

"Lara, they will." His voice raised an octave, and Kamia stirred. Boss covered his mouth. "Sorry," he whispered.

Boss turned the meat and moved closer to Lara. "Are you cold?"

"A little."

He put his arm around her, and she laid her head on his shoulder. "I'm scared."

"I know. I am, too. But we got She-woman over there. If worse comes to worst, I'll send her out to kill another boar."

Lara loved the feel of his warm body against hers. "She's something else, isn't she?"

"She sure is." Boss leaned his head on hers. "I want to apologize for how I treated you."

"What do you mean?" She knew exactly what he meant, but she wanted to hear him say it.

"It was Isa. I've never gotten over her. I just couldn't bring myself to get into a relationship with you. I liked you. I mean, I still do. And I guess that scared me."

"What happened?"

Boss pulled some meat off the fire and added more. Laying the pieces on a pile of leaves to cool, he began his story. "Isa and I met at a party on the island. A couple of guys and I were invited to a pig roast. With nothing better to do, we went. The moment I saw her, I was in love. I don't know how to explain it, but it was truly love-at-first-sight. Isa means rainbow, and she was the brightest, most colorful part of my life."

He picked up a stick and made circles in the sand. "We married against the wishes of her family. Her people were, and most likely still are, very superstitious. They said bringing a white man into the family would bring bad luck to them."

"Bad luck? Really?"

"If you think about it, it was entirely true. I brought bad luck to Isa."

"Boss—"

"No, let me finish. Isa knew that if she married me, they would ban her from her community, her family. And still, she did. For an entire year, we lived in Navy housing and our love grew stronger than ever. But Isa missed her family. She was the fifth child of eight kids. Family means everything to them. Isa had longed to keep in touch with them, but even her brothers and sisters would not communicate with her. Not as long as she stayed married to me."

"That's not fair." Lara couldn't imagine such a culture that would abandon a family member for falling in love.

"I didn't think so either. When my enlistment was up, I wanted Isa to come with me back to the states. I was up for shore duty and had landed a nice billet on the submarine base in San Diego. She wouldn't come with me. She was convinced if she went back home to her family, they would take her back. I begged her to let them go and come with me. She told me that marrying me was a mistake, and that she had to go back to them and beg their forgiveness.

"With nothing else to stay in the Navy for, I terminated my orders to San Diego and put in my discharge papers. She didn't leave right away. She waited until my enlistment was up. I want to believe she loved me enough to change her mind, but three days before I was due to go back to the states, I came home from work, and she was gone. I tried to go back to her village and speak with her, but her brothers and sisters stood up to me and I had no choice but to back down. I was up for an honorable discharge that would have quickly turned dishonorable if I'd picked a fight with the locals. So, I gave up the fight and left. As hard as it was for me to leave Isa behind, I walked away. But I saw her. Tears filled her eyes as she cried for her loss. I know she loved me. She just couldn't give up her family."

"Then why is Kamia not with her relatives? What happened?"

"That's what I don't understand. Isa's family had accepted her back into the village. I don't know why—"

"It was me." Kamia sat up and rubbed her eyes. "I am the reason they banned her. I'm a half-breed. My blood is tainted. They threw my mother out because of me."

"Oh, Kamia." Lara's heart broke for the girl. "I'm so sorry."

"I'm not. They were cruel to my mother and me. Threw stones at us if we came too close. Only one of them ever helped us. My Uncle Guaiya. He visited us often and brought me gifts. But no one could know, so we kept it secret."

"I'm glad you had your uncle there for you," Lara said. "He cared for you."

"Guaiya means love. Nana was his favorite. But Guaiya died, and we were on our own again."

"Did your mother ever tell you about me?" Boss did not look at the girl. Instead, he continued making circles in the sand.

"Nana said you were a good man. She said her love for her family was too strong to go with you until you were gone. When she found out she was pregnant with me, she wanted to contact you, but she was afraid you would reject her as her family did."

Lara wanted to ask how her mother died, but thought maybe it was just too much for Kamia to talk about with it being so fresh. Instead, she tried to change the subject. "Are you hungry, Kamia? There is meat cooked."

"No. I am fine. You should get some sleep, Mames. Morning comes too soon."

Lara didn't miss that Kamia directed all her words to her and avoided her father unless she had something sarcastic to say. She was sure Boss didn't miss that either.

Boss yawned. "Yeah, why don't you get some sleep, Mames. I'll keep watch until morning."

"Just a couple hours," Lara agreed. "But when I wake up, it will be your turn to sleep, promise me."

"Okay. I promise. Get some sleep."

Kamia laid back down and was back asleep before Lara had the chance to stand. "I'm sorry, Callan." It was the first time she'd called him by his given name, and she liked the way it flowed off her tongue. It sounded much more personal.

Boss put a warm hand to her face and leaned in close. Lara's insides did flips at the thought of his lips so close to hers. And he didn't stop. He came closer until his lips touched hers. "You are beautiful," he whispered just before his hand came around her neck and he pulled her into a warm kiss.

It was not a passionate kiss, but Lara's body responded as if it was. Goosebumps ran over her arms, and her heart raced.

"I better get some sleep."

Boss ran his fingers through her hair. His blue eyes connected with hers and penetrated her soul. He leaned in again and kissed her. The taste of his salty lips was more than she could handle and she pulled back.

"I'm sorry." She jumped up. "I better go."

Tripping over the pile of kindling behind her, she righted herself before she fell flat on her face. She didn't look back but kept walking toward the shelter. She'd have rather slept next to Kamia, but she needed her space. At that moment, any wild animal was safer than being close to him. He was a hazard to her heart.

Lying on the makeshift bed Boss had built of palm fronds covered with his own clothing, she closed her eyes but could not sleep. The musky scent of cologne that wafted from his clothes awakened her senses as she thought about his lips against hers, invading her territory. Breaking down her walls. Tearing her heart into pieces.

Before falling asleep, she vowed to keep her distance from him. He loved Isa. He'd said all the right words, apologized for his retreat from her and was being more than kind, but Lara was not Isa. She could not fill the hole in his heart that the woman left. She was only a convenience, a warm body in the middle of nowhere. Her heart felt as deserted as the island they were trapped on.

Yawning, she closed her eyes and allowed herself to drift off to sleep.

❦

Boss sat out in the open air, staring at the fire as it died down. The meat they'd cooked filled the air with a sweet aroma. He'd wrapped it in the leaves, as his survivalist daughter had suggested, and looked out into the early morning sunrise.

If he hadn't been stranded, he'd have thought it an amazing scene. The quiet was serene. The only noise, the crackle of the fire that smoldered down to nothing, and the light breathing of his daughter sleeping comfortably by the fire.

He'd checked on Lara several times and each time found her sleeping soundly with his oversized Raiders jersey draped over the top of her. He'd loved to have crawled into the poorly built shelter, but needed to keep watch. Besides that, if Lara found him curled up next to her, he'd likely get punched.

His eyes fought against the burn to close them. Only another hour before the sun would be high enough in the sky to see the area fully.

Getting onto his feet, Boss made his way to the ocean where they'd left his suitcase full of wild boar. After tying several wires together to make an extension long enough to get the case deep into the water, he hoped it was still there, and the meat was not spoiled.

As he made his way closer to the beach, an object floated off in the distance. With the sun growing higher in the sky, it cast a blinding light on the object. Boss waded into the water. The closer he got, the clearer the bright purple top of Lara's plastic top luggage became. Splashing the chilled water all over his clothes, he waded out further to the baggage. At least if they were going to be stuck for a while, they'd have more belongings to go around.

The water got deeper as he went, and soon he was swimming to get a hold of it. The further he swam, the further out the luggage went. Realizing he was pushing it further out with each wave he created, he slowed his pace. When he finally got close enough to reach out and touch it, he was exhausted. He grabbed the handle and held tight to the case. Boss swam back to shore using the case as a sort of floatation device. It didn't work so well, as the case sank under his weight. Once he had a firm footing in the sand, he dragged it from the water and sat on the shore to catch his breath. With the weight of it, he was pretty sure her luggage was not waterproof. That was okay. Their belongings would dry. Now all they needed to do was find fresh water. That was the priority for the day. After that, he would try to make a better shelter to keep them safe from the island inhabitants.

He dragged it up through the sand, water seeping out through the sides, making it lighter as he went. Lara and Kamia were rekindling the fire as he walked up. Seeing them up and about made his exhaustion subside. Lara bent over the fire wearing his black jersey. It fell around her knees, making it look like a cute dress. Easily, it looked better on her than it did on him. With a sigh, he continued his pace. He didn't know what it was with these two girls that made his heart ache to be a part of their lives. But the yearning for a complete family was strong.

"What's that?" Kamia asked as he got closer.

Lara looked up. "My luggage!" she cried and ran to him. Giving him a hug big enough to about knock him over, he fell dramatically to the ground. She, on top of him. Lara giggled, but then their eyes met, and she stopped. Her face became serious. He did everything he could to not lean his head up to her face and kissing her.

"What are you two doing over there?" Kamia asked.

The look in Lara's eyes left, and she smiled. "Thank you," she said, standing and grabbing her bag. "Sorry I didn't wake up to relieve you. I guess I was more tired than I thought."

"No problem." He extended his hand for help up. She ignored him, turned around, and dragged her bag away.

"Hey! A little help here?"

Lara turned and grinned at him and kept walking toward the fire.

"Don't mind me," he called. "It's not like I just found your only clothes!"

She giggled and continued her alluring walk in his jersey. "Thanks, Boss," she called. "I'm so happy you swam two miles out to retrieve my luggage." Still, she didn't turn. He watched her walk. She had no idea just how beautiful she was.

Boss got up and shook off the sand. Brushing himself off, he turned back to the ocean, remembering what he'd gone out there to do.

"I'll be back," he called.

"Wait!" Kamia said, dropped her sticks, and ran towards him. "I want to come with you."

Boss waited for the fifteen-year-old to reach him, barefoot, and wearing another of his tee-shirts on top of her old, dirty shorts. She made it to him, a bit out of breath.

"You think it's still there?" he asked.

"I hope so. If not, I can fish later today. But first, we must find fresh water."

"My thoughts exactly," he said.

Once they reached the tree he'd tied his makeshift cord to, he tugged on it. "Too loose," he said, pulling the wire easily from the ocean.

"I bet a shark got it," Kamia said.

"They don't come that close to shore, do they?"

"Not normally, but I fear they might have smelled the meat."

"I hear sharks can smell one drop of blood from a mile away."

He pulled at the cord until nothing came up but the end. No suitcase. Nothing.

"I knew it!" Kamia cried, but quickly pepped up. "It's okay. I will kill another one. It's no problem."

"No problem for you. That was an expensive suitcase!" He feigned anger.

"Oh, poor baby," she answered as her face became serious. "That is the least of our worries."

"You're right. Let's get some breakfast and do some hiking. There's got to be fresh water on this island somewhere." He untied the wires from the tree and wrapped them around his hand.

"Or not."

"What do you mean?" He turned to her.

"Why does no one live here?"

She had a point. "But the greenery is plush. There has to be fresh water, right?"

He spoke to her as an equal because she had proved herself much smarter than the average fifteen-year-old. At least in survival techniques.

"Right. If there is a spring somewhere, Lara and I will find it."

Boss turned to her. "What do you mean, you and Lara?"

"You need some sleep, Boss." She lowered her brows. "You have been up all night."

It sounded strange to hear her call him by his nickname. What would he prefer? Dad? They'd only known each other for a week. He wouldn't push her. "I don't feel comfortable sleeping while the two of you wander aimlessly in the jungle."

"You will be of no help if you are exhausted. I will keep your girl-friend safe." She pulled his army knife from her shorts pocket and flipped it open.

"She's not my —" There was no use arguing with a teenager. He would not win. "Give me a couple of hours of sleep, and we can all go together."

"We need to find water soon. None of us have had a drink—"

"Fine. Just be careful. I will get a couple of hours and head out to find you. Please be careful."

He trusted in his daughter's ability and island awareness more than his own. Still, he worried for her and for Lara. He had an idea that as soon as he fell asleep, and he did need sleep, that the two bull-headed women would go off without him, anyway. There was no use telling them not to.

"I have started on some spears. I will finish them off before we leave, but you underestimate your girlfriend."

"She's really not my girlfriend." Boss headed back to the camp. Kamia followed behind.

"The way you watch her every move says differently." She rushed off past him without allowing him to respond.

"I do not look... I'm just worried about her," he called after her. "Really!"

She shook her head and picked up her pace. He hadn't convinced her, and to be honest, he hadn't convinced himself either. He'd been attracted to the woman ever since he'd met her. But Isa...

He picked up his pace to catch up with her. As soon as they rounded the bend, Lara came into view. She was pulling her clothes out of her bag and placing them around the already warm sand.

"They aren't very wet," she said as they came closer. "Hardly even damp."

He figured as much, since, if too much water had gotten in, the bag would have sunk to the bottom of the ocean.

"Good." He grabbed a seat on the sand next to the fire. "Now I can have my jersey back."

Lara stood. "But I like it." She smoothed it down over her shorts and gave him a pouty look.

Boss rolled his eyes. It was no hard feat to give in to her. She looked good in it. "Means you have to become a Raider's fan."

"Who says I'm not?"

Boss rolled his eyes again. "I've got to get some sleep. Tarzan over here insists on the two of you going out in the jungle on a quest for fresh water. I told her it's not—"

"Good idea, Kamia. We are going to need something to drink soon. Coconuts are not doing it for me."

Boss sighed. He preferred not to be ganged up on by two girls, but he wouldn't be much use to them with no sleep. "Fine. Please, be careful."

It was debatable if he would get any rest with them out of his sight. He closed his eyes to stave off the burning. He was no spring chicken, anymore. Mid watches were certainly not as easy as they used to be.

Kamia sat whittling away at her second spear. "You should go into the shelter," she said without looking up. "If I have to chase down another boonie pig, he might run out this way."

Boss rolled his eyes. "You think I can't take on a wild boar?"

"Awake and unarmed? No. And definitely not in your sleep."

She had a point. Why did she always have a point? Boss raised his hands in defeat, stood to his feet, and headed for the shelter. "If you get bludgeoned by a pig, don't come crying to me."

Lara laughed. He looked back, and her face assumed a look of worry. "Can you be bludgeoned by a wild boar?"

Boss laughed. "Nah, they are more afraid of you than you are of them. I'm the only one who has to worry." He yawned. "I'll be the defenseless sleeping one."

An object flew through the air, just missing his feet. He looked down to see a spear stuck in the sand next to him.

"That will keep you safe," Kamia called. "Keep it under your pillow."

Pillow? Pshh. If only he were back in his home with his pillow top mattress. He picked up the spear. "Thanks, Kamia. I'll keep it close."

8

"And one for you." Kamia tossed a sharpened spear to Lara.

As it fell to her feet, she stared at it. "Is this necessary?" she asked, knowing it was.

Kamia nodded. "There's probably not much worse than boonie pigs, but there are birds on the island, so you know what that means, right?"

She had no idea. "No, what?"

"Birds can bring snakes and other animals onto an island from nearby habitations. Which means, there's a good chance there are snakes on the island."

"Poisonous snakes?"

"Could be. Most likely, just brown tree snakes." She picked up the last spear.

"Are those poisonous?"

"Yep." Kamia slipped on her sandals and headed for the trees.

Snakes to Lara were a fear as bad, if not worse, than flying. "Wait." She rushed after Kamia. "What if I get bit? Will I die?" The thought of slow death, as the poison took over her body, made her cringe. A blue line of snake venom making its way to stop her heart.

Kamia kept walking. Lara stood at the edge of the trees. "Kamia!"

"You won't die," she answered without turning. "Unless you are a two-year-old."

A rush of relief came over her, and she hurried to catch up. "Why?"

"Brown tree snakes emit a poison, but their venomous teeth are at the back of their mouth. They use them to stun lizards and other small creatures so they can eat them. He would have to gnaw on you for a bit before injecting enough venom in you to even make you sick."

She thanked God she was not a child. Feeling a little braver, she followed.

"They are very aggressive though, so don't go poking around with your spear."

And the fear was back. "How aggressive?"

"Highly. And they like to lunge."

"Great." Lara was rethinking her decision to go out in the jungle alone without Boss. "Maybe we should wait for Boss."

"Boss cannot save us. He may be smart, but he does not have survival skills."

Lara couldn't disagree. Neither of them possessed the training to live under such circumstances.

They walked further into the jungle, creating a trail as they tramped through the trees.

A good fifteen minutes later, Lara began slapping at her arms. Something was biting her, and she was sure it was mosquitoes. "What should we—"

"Shhh," Kamia waved her hands behind her back to quiet Lara and leaned forward. "You hear that?"

What? A brown tree snake? Did they actually live in the trees? A *boar?* Her imagination took off on a wild goose chase.

"Water. It's far off, but I can hear the rush of water."

Kamia continued forward, but as hard as she tried, Lara could hear nothing past the sound of her own feet crunching on the ground below. Her eyes shifted from area to area, watching for snakes or boars.

"Can you hear it?" Kamia whispered. "Up ahead."

She still could not hear it. The girl had bionic ears. She followed vigilantly, not wanting to be too far away from the female Tarzan. Hearing a sound comparable to water streaming into a bathtub made her stop. "I hear it!" Excitement ran through her.

"Shhh," Kamia spoke, moving closer to the glorious sound. The foliage grew greener and thicker with each step until they could hardly take a step forward. The trees formed a barrier around their beloved source of water.

"How are we going to get through that?" Lara whispered.

Kamia moved forward. Pressing her body between the trees, she squeezed to the other side. Lara watched through the trees.

"Come on. You can make it."

"I'm not as small or as flexible as you." Lara sighed and walked toward the minuscule entrance. Looking through, she saw a paradise. The sight of a waterfall crashing down into the stream below was magnificent.

"It's just like the falls we visited before we left Guam." She stared in awe, still from the jungle side of the trees.

"Talofofo." Kamia bent down. "It's fresh. Come on, Mames. Slide in. The water is cool." The girl cupped water in her hands and brought it to her mouth.

Lara's mouth watered. "Okay, I'll try."

She pushed through until she had only an arm and leg on the other side. "I'm too big." Lara didn't consider herself voluptuous by any means, but she wasn't a size zero like the girl enjoying the water on the other side.

Kamia stood. Her face brightened in amusement. Lara was stuck. Her face reddened at her predicament. Her hip was wedged so tight between the two trees that she couldn't seem to push the rest of her body through.

"Uh, a little help here?"

"What do you want me to do?" Kamia asked. By that time, her hand covered her mouth, and her eyes gleamed with laughter.

"This is not funny!" Lara pulled at her waist. Ugh. The disparities of having a figure.

"Here." Kamia came towards her. "I'll pull you through."

The thought of getting more of her body stuck was frightening. "No! Push me back."

Kamia was laughing so hard she almost fell several times trying to get to Lara.

Lara pulled and tugged some more, but her body wouldn't budge. A rustling sounded from behind, and she couldn't turn her head to look and see what it was.

The sound came closer. Terrified, she pushed through. Screaming, she landed on the other side, lost her footing, and fell straight into the water with a splash. Kamia bent over, water dripping from her hair and face, laughing so hard Lara couldn't help but laugh herself.

"You think it's funny?" Lara jumped up, grabbed the sleeve of Kamia's shirt, and fell backward, bringing Kamia into the refreshing water with her. The two splashed and played like kids in the community pool on the first day of summer.

Another rustle sounded, and they stopped and stared toward the trees. "Can they get through?" Lara whispered. Surely, they had a way to the freshwater. They had to drink, too. Holding her breath, she listened.

Before Kamia could answer, a voice rang out. "Lara! Kamia!" Boss rushed up to the trees, scaring any boonie pig within miles. "Where are you?"

"Over here!" Lara cried out.

Boss ran up to the trees and looked through. "Oh, thank God. I heard a scream and thought—"

"We found fresh water," Kamia rang out, splashing up at him.

"Good." He stood back and looked at the opening. "How in the world did you get through there?"

Offended for a moment, she brushed it off. "Easy, when you're about to be dinner for a wild boar."

Boss put a hand through the narrow opening and then pulled it back out. "Not getting in through there."

He disappeared as Kamia and Lara made their way out of the water and sat down on the side, basking in the warm sun.

"Gimme a cabin and Wi-Fi, and I'd never leave," Lara said.

"It is peaceful. Untouched. Maybe we could build a house here and stay?" Her eyes gleamed with hopefulness.

"Don't you want to meet a man someday and fall in love? The only one here is your father."

"Yuck." She crinkled her nose. "I had a boyfriend, well, he was just a friend, but I liked him, and I think he liked me."

"What's his name?"

"Puengi. He's sixteen. I will miss him."

"I'm sorry, Kamia." It was no use telling her she would find another. She would, but Lara knew the pain of losing someone you love. First her mother and now her boyfriend. Too much hurt for one young girl. They sat, staring out at the water. *Why does life have to be so painful?*

Minutes later, Boss made his way back to them through another, obviously wider, entrance. "Opening's back that way." He pointed a thumb in the direction he came from. There's a bit of a trail as well. Probably from the wildlife coming to and from."

"Get a drink," Lara said. "It's fresh and tastes great."

"Not after you two mongrels have jumped in and contaminated it." He chuckled.

Kamia reached down and splashed water at him, and he jumped back too late. Water splashed onto his jean shorts, soaking the bottom and his legs.

"Feisty." He sat down between them.

"I thought you were sleeping," Lara said.

"I was until I heard screaming." He yawned. "'Bout scared me to death. Knocked my head on the top of the wing trying to get out."

"Sorry, I thought I was about to become dinner for a boonie pig."

"Good to see you in one piece," he answered, as he bent down to splash some water on his face. "What's for lunch?"

Kamia pulled the knife out of her pocket. "Pig?"

"You and that knife." Boss shook his head. "I saw some wild berries on the way here. Maybe we can catch a couple of fish to go with it."

Kamia shrugged and put the knife back in her pocket. "Suit your-self." Slipping off her shoes, she headed toward the trees.

"Where you going?"

She continued her pace without comment.

"What's she doing now?"

Lara shrugged.

Within seconds, Kamia was shimmying up a coconut tree.

Boss grabbed the waist of his shorts, and looking down he said, "How'd she get my belt?"

Once at the top, Kamia threw down a couple of coconuts. Lara and Boss stood to catch them.

She shimmied back down, handed Boss his belt and slipped back on her shoes. "We can use the shells to carry some water back. It won't be much, but better than nothing."

"Hm." Boss clucked his tongue. "Good idea."

Kamia put Lara and Boss to shame as she showed off her expert skills in fishing. Kamia had speared three, and he'd missed many more. Boss couldn't help but wonder if he and Lara might be dead by now if it weren't for Kamia. He thought about the fishing poles sitting in the back of his closet. Those would have come in handy.

On a sharp rock, Kamia broke each coconut in two. She pulled out the inner core and went to work shaving out the nut from inside, eating pieces as she went.

"Want some?" She handed Lara a slice, ignoring Boss.

"Sure, I'll take some." Boss reached around and took a piece and popped it into his mouth.

"Hey that was mine," Lara said.

"Well, apparently you get special privileges with the girl, so I gotta take what I can get."

Still ignoring him, Kamia cut another piece for Lara.

Boss chuckled. "Get no respect around here." He was only teasing his daughter. Trying to pull her out of her shell.

Kamia continued to core the coconut, handing off pieces to Lara and ignoring Boss. When finally she finished, she handed her master-piece to Boss. He took it and inspected it. With just a thin layer of meat left inside, it would be strong enough to hold plenty of water.

"Thanks. My first gift from my daughter," he joked, but he truly was grateful.

"You are welcome. It's the only one you get."

"The only coconut bowl or the only gift?"

"Both." She cracked another coconut open and began carving out another bowl. Boss didn't miss the playful grin on her face. He'd wear on her.

When she had three bowls finished, they filled them with water, and Boss showed them the way he'd gotten into the area without having to squeeze through trees. The thought of Lara pressing her body through that tight opening made him smile. That would have been a sight to see.

When they made it back to camp, a good deal of the water they'd each held had splashed out. Still, it would be enough to sip on as the day got longer. His first plan was to build a better shelter for the three of them to sleep in.

He set about cutting palm fronds, but before he'd got many, the sky rumbled, signifying it was about to rain. With almost no warning, a downpour hit the island. It was a warm rain and felt good on his sweaty body. He watched as Lara and Kamia scurried to keep the fire going. Try as they might, it was no use. Soon smoke rose, making the two of them pant and cough. The fish, not fully cooked, was now smoking.

"Lania!" Kamia yelled as she grabbed the fish from the smoke.

Boss stared at his daughter as she struggled in frustration. He knew what that Chamorro word meant, and it wasn't nice.

Kamia looked his way and covered her mouth. "Sorry!" she called.

Boss chuckled. Isa had a bit of a potty-mouth herself. His daughter had undoubtedly gotten her temper, along with her colorful use of words, from her mother.

No sooner had the rain started than it was finished, leaving everything soaking wet. The sun came out, pretending it hadn't just allowed that rush of water to ruin their progress. Looking over at Lara's suitcase, which was now filled with rainwater, he had an idea.

"You think you two could walk back to the waterfall without getting eaten by boonie pigs?" he called. He knew Kamia could keep herself safe in the jungle. It was Lara he worried more about.

"I don't know," Lara said, pulling her wet hair back from her face. "I'm deathly afraid of meeting one of those dreaded brown tree snakes."

He hadn't thought about those buggers since his last tour on Guam. The brown tree snake population had about ruined the island's ecosystem. They were an irritating bunch, popping up in toilets and sink drains at random. Often, they made their way into the electrical system, shutting down the power completely. He hated snakes.

"Grab your spear," Kamia recommended to Lara. "What would you like us to do?"

Boss walked over to Lara's suitcase and with his knife, he snapped it into two separate pieces.

"Hey, that's my luggage. What are you doing?"

He poured the rainwater from one side into the other. "We can use this, but we will need more. Think you could fill this with water? Maybe if you each grabbed a side, we could get some more fresh water to wash and bathe in?"

"Oh," Lara said. "Good idea."

"Maybe while we are gone, you could get that side panel off the wing, and we could use it to cook on," Kamia said. Had he imagined it, or was this the first full sentence she'd directed at him since they left the island? He could work with that.

"Oh," Boss said, echoing Lara's words. "Good idea."

The girls left with the suitcase between them and their spears at their side. Boss couldn't help thinking how cute Lara looked with her hair all ragged and wet, holding a spear in her hand. Primal was the word that came to mind. He liked it.

Grabbing the knife Kamia left by the still smoking fire pit, Boss headed to the wing and snapped off the flapper panel. It would need to be well sterilized in the fire, but it would make a great skillet. Much better than the charred meat they'd eaten without it.

He delved into the forest to grab several long sticks. Tying them together with vines, he made a makeshift holder for the metal plate. Taking pride in his work, he set the flapper on top and stood back. Perfect. That was as long as no one kicked it over. Changing his mind, feeling it was much too high, he grabbed a rock and banged them into the soft sand. He then grabbed more rocks and towered them around his creation. Pulling a little on them, he decided, even a strong kick wouldn't pull it down.

Happy with his creation, he set off to finish snapping palm fronds from the lower trees. It didn't take him long to find a couple of toppled over trees to make a lean-to out of. He dragged four of them back to camp, skinned the branches and pressed them into the ground as far as he could.

He sat down for a minute and rested. Sweat was so thick on his body that his shirt stuck to his chest. The humidity was at an all-time high after the rain. After drinking the last of his water, he stood and went back into the jungle to find two more beams to use as cross-posts for the roof. Never having to create something so extensive before, he was surprised at his own ingenuity.

Once back at the camp, he grabbed the wires that had failed him in the underwater suitcase venture and tied the roof logs to the uprights and stood back to admire his work. Sweat dripped into his eyes and he wiped it away with his shirt. He was exhausted after less than an hour's sleep before running to their rescue, only to find them splashing and playing in the refreshing water.

He sat for only a minute before forcing himself to get up and continue working. Making quick work of the job, he began throwing palm fronds on the top, tying them to the cross beams as he went. By the time he finished, he'd made a crude, yet big enough for three, shelter with palm fronds on the top, sticks, and brush on the sides and a towel from Lara's belongings over the door. He set out, tying up as much as he could to keep the thing intact. The shelter looked quite stable. Laying down more fronds inside, and covering it with more clothes, Boss relaxed back and admired his work from the inside.

9

"This thing is heavy," Lara said as the weight of the filled suitcase pulled on her back.

Water splashed over the sides, but at least they would have something to wash up in once they got it back. She wouldn't dare drink it, but the fresh water wasn't far from the camp. Not to mention coconut milk was even closer.

"Almost there," Kamia encouraged. "Then I go back to get a pig."

"Are you serious?" Lara looked across at the girl. She was serious. "Boss said we should stick to fish."

"Do you want to eat fish for the rest of our stay?"

"But Boss said—"

"Boss is just trying to look out for me, but I have hunted all my life. My mother taught me how to survive. We only had each other, and now she is gone, and I am stuck with this... this... Boss. What kind of name is that, anyway? He's not my boss."

"You're right, Kamia." Lara kept her pace on the thin trail they'd made coming back and forth. "He is only looking out for you, just as your mother did. He's your father."

"I was a burden to my mother. I refuse to be a burden to him, too. I can take care of myself."

"Why do you say that? What happened to your mom?" Maybe it wasn't the right time, but the girl seemed to have a chip on her shoulder that she wanted to offload. In her experience, it was much better to carry a load when you had help. Lara said a small prayer for Kamia. *Open her heart, Lord.*

"You know why. They cast my mother away from her family because of me." Kamia said the words Lara already knew but did not answer the question of what happened to her mother. Maybe it was too early. Before she could contemplate pushing the issue, Kamia answered.

"I don't know what happened to her. She got very sick. I tried to nurse her back to health, but she wasn't getting better. No matter what I tried... she wouldn't... she died." Sadness reached the girl's eyes, and as much as Lara did not want to stop in the middle of the jungle, with wild pigs and snakes, she hurt for the girl.

"Let's set this down and rest for a minute."

Kamia complied. A short distance away was a felled tree. Lara brushed the dirt off, scoured the area for predators, then sat down. Kamia followed suit.

"There was no hospital to bring her to?"

"She got too sick, too fast. I didn't know how to get her help." Kamia stared down at the ground and shuffled her hands. "Before she died, she told me about my father. The first time she ever spoke of him. That's when I found my birth certificate and got a ride to the Navy base. I was scared. I couldn't make it without her. I never wanted—"

"You shouldn't have to deal with that. I'm sorry you have had a rough life. If Boss, your father, would have known about you, I'm sure he would have come for you sooner."

"You don't see. I didn't go to the base to find my father. I went to find refuge. My mother told me they could find me a place to live. That we are a U.S. territory, and they have funds to help. She never accepted government help, but she wanted me to try. I didn't mean for them to call him. I only wanted help."

Lara placed her arm around Kamia's shoulder. "Sometimes God

brings help in a form you don't think you need, but I assure you, your father is a good man. He is all the help you need."

"Then why is he so bossy? He thinks I am a child."

"It's just his nature. And well, if you don't mind my saying so, I think you inherited a little of that bossiness from him."

Kamia smiled. "Maybe."

"Maybe?" Lara squeezed the girl's shoulder. "To be honest, I wasn't happy with your father myself. But now that I know him better, I think he's got a lot of pain in his past that he wasn't ready to deal with. I think you entering his life is going to better help him deal with it."

"My mother?"

"I think so. I don't know what transpired between them before your father left, but I think your mother left him with a hole the size of the Grand Canyon in his heart."

"He likes you."

Lara liked him. She liked him a lot, but there was just too much hurt between them to ever make something of it. "I like him, too. But sometimes we have to wrestle with our own demons before God can make a way to love again."

"Maybe." Kamia stood. "He better get rid of those demons quickly."

"God is working on him," *and me.* "I think you are the salve he needs to patch up that big hole in his heart."

"Gigantic." Kamia chuckled. "Like the Grand Canyon."

"Yup." Lara stood. "Let's get this water back to camp before the tree snakes come out."

They lifted the suitcase and continued their trek back to camp. Lara realized she'd been speaking to herself as much as to Kamia. Boss had been hurt much more than the jerk from Texas had hurt her. He'd been in love. Real love. Something she'd yet to find. She worried that all the attention he'd been pouring on her was not real, that he was tired, and emotional, and — stranded. She was his only option here, and his actions back home had already proved she had been only a passing phase. Yeah, he'd apologized for that. Sorry or not, it would take a lot more than that for Lara to give her heart away again. Lara brought her focus back to the present. Kamia.

"I have a book I want you to read when we get back. It's called *Pilgrim's Progress.*"

"I can't."

"Sure you — wait." Lara turned back to Kamia with a quickness that made a wave of water splash onto the jungle floor. "Have you never been to school?"

Kamia shook her head. "I know only a little bit. My mother used to read to me from a Bible. It was his. The only thing she kept from her past. She carried it around with her wherever she went."

"Your father's? How do you know?"

"She told me. When she was dying. She said it was from my father. That's where I found my birth certificate."

"I bet that was important to her. It's hard to let go of the ones we love."

"Yes. But now it's at the bottom of the sea. I used to try reading the words, and I cherished it because my mother did, but I didn't know who he was. Only that it was important to her."

Lara turned and continued her pace. How could a girl reach the age of fifteen and not know how to read? Guam was a US territory. Did they not hold to the same education system? Were there other children who could not read and write? Did Kamia merely slip through the cracks? Those were questions that surely needed to be answered, but Lara did not think she would find them. And that hurt. How would the girl make it in a California public school? Would she be thrown into the special education system? Kamia would not stand for that. She was too stubborn. Lara decided she would teach the girl herself. At least the basics. She would not give up until Kamia was as book smart as she was street smart.

As they made it back to camp, with most of the water intact and a good sheen of sweat on their brows, Boss was nowhere in sight. Kamia, seemingly not interested in where he was, began clearing away the ashy remains of the fire that had been snuffed out. Kamia inspected the contraption around the fire that Boss had made to hold up the jet flap. She looked impressed with his work but did not feel the need to mention it. Complimenting her father, even if he weren't there to hear it, might mean she'd accepted him. And from her own admittance, that was a step she wasn't ready to take. Still, the girl was on her way to making peace with her father. Quickly, Kamia set wood inside the pit and started the fire.

Glancing around, Lara spotted a crudely built structure in the same spot she'd slept in the night before.

"What is that?" Kamia asked.

"I think it's our new home. For now."

Kamia giggled. "He's done it all wrong. It will fall over at the first strong wind."

Lara smiled and pulled up her flowered beach towel from the entry to see Boss sleeping soundly inside his ramshackle hut. She had to admit it looked quite sturdy. At the very least, it would protect them from the outside creatures. She replaced the towel and headed back to the pit where Kamia was starting a new fire. She was getting hungry, and the fish were beginning to stink. They would not be edible.

"I will go catch another pig." Kamia stood and grabbed her spear. "We need to eat." She shrugged as if it was no big deal to catch and kill a wild boar, and rushed off back into the jungle.

Lara could have tried to stop her, but after what the girl said about being a burden, she couldn't do it. Instead, she sat down by the fire and prayed for her safety. Boss would be mad when he found out, but there was nothing she could do about that. Instead, she kept the fire going. It was out in the open, and eventually, someone was bound to see it and come to save them. That was if they were even looking for them yet.

Chandler and Dena were off on their anniversary, and it would still be almost another week before they would call Boss to pick them up. The thought of spending four to five more days on the island made her ill. She was not cut out for island life. She didn't even like camping. And this whole boar and snake thing, it was too much. Lara popped a wild berry into her mouth. It was the only edible thing left from their lunch. It was juicy and sweet, and Kamia had assured her it was not poisonous.

Half an hour later, a squeal sounded off in the jungle and Lara knew what that meant. Another pig had met its doom. Another fifteen minutes later, Kamia came back to camp dragging lunch behind her.

"Nice," Lara said, even though her insides squirmed over the thought of gutting another dead animal.

Kamia dropped the pig next to her and sat. "Not as big as the last, but this time we have daylight on our side. If I can get this stripped and hung, we will have dried meat by morning."

"Need help?" Lara asked, hoping Kamia would say she didn't.

"Sure. You can help me gut him."

Ugh.

"We can use the hide to cover that shelter thing he made. Speaking of, where is he?"

"Sleeping in that shelter thing he made. We better let him sleep."

"Yes. Let the sleeping bear rest. We don't need his help."

"I looked inside. It's a pretty sturdy shelter." She hoped to get Kamia to agree that her father was good for something.

"Psh. You wait. First big wind."

So much for that. Lara held her breath and settled in to help Kamia gut the pig and turn its meat into strips to be hung out to dry. It was a daunting task, but as *The Little Red Hen* said, if you don't help bake the bread you don't get to help eat it. Surely bread would be less disgusting than gutting a pig. Still, she helped.

"Are you excited yet about going to California with your father?" Lara asked, hoping the girl had changed her stance on the issue, and foremost, to distract herself from her bloody task.

"No, not really. I don't think I will fit in so well."

"I didn't exactly fit in where I lived either. As a white girl in the projects, I took a lot of ridicule from a lot of kids, but I made my way. I'm sure you will, too."

"What's it like there?" Kamia worked steadily on the pig.

"California has a vast population. There are people of all kinds. You will find where you fit in easily." She stopped for a moment. "Kamia, I'd like to teach you to read and write. Would you like that?"

"I'm too old to learn those things."

"You are never too old to learn. God has a hand in every situation, and He will help you through it. I get that it would be hard for a teenager in the public school system to learn the basics, while others are preparing for college, but Kamia, you can do and be anything you want to."

"God has not been so good to me. My mother believed. Her family was Catholic. She always tried to tell me about Him, but I didn't want to… How can I believe in a God who let this happen to me?"

That was the age-old question that no one seemed to have a definitive answer for. Still, Lara tried. "Did your mother read to you the story in the Bible about Adam and Eve, the first humans created?"

"She did. But I don't get what that has to do with us." Kamia stopped her work and sat back.

"Would you allow me to retell it the way I understand it?"

Kamia nodded.

As she cut strips of meat, Lara told her story. "Adam and Eve were the first humans God created. He created them to walk with Him. They had no shame, no troubles, no sin. It was a beautiful existence between them and God. But, with everything in life, God had one rule. That rule was for them not to touch the one tree in the garden out of all the other trees. God gave them a vast array of fruit trees, vegetable gardens, all the food they ever could want. That was their only restriction."

"And they disobeyed," Kamia smoothed the sand beneath her with her palm.

"Yep."

"So, why did God even put that tree there in the first place, if He didn't want them to eat from it?"

"That's a great question. I have pondered that myself. The truth is, we cannot understand all of God's ways, but I believe it was put there to give them an option. The fruit from that very tree and only that tree would give them the ability to see all the things of the world. That's why it was called *The Tree of Knowledge of Good and Evil*. God knew there would be evil in the world. He'd cast the devil from heaven and Satan was on the warpath, so to speak. He wasn't happy that God had cast him out. So, you see, there was sin even before our world existed."

Kamia's eyes met Lara's. Was she reaching her?

She continued. "So, no matter the reason God placed that tree there, Adam and Eve had the option to obey or disobey. When tempted by Satan, Eve was fascinated by the lie the serpent told her. She wanted to be like God. To know all, see all, and be a god herself. The moment she took a bite of that fruit, sin entered the world. There was no more quiet communion with God. From that moment on God promised the world would see toil and despair."

"But, why? If he hadn't tempted them with the tree —"

"I know, I get it, Kamia. I do. And for many years I missed the point, just as you are now. Even in this fallen world of pain and heartache, God wants a relationship with you. He wants you to see through all the hate and evil and find goodness. Despite what you see, God is love. Look at us here, stranded on this—"

A voice spoke from behind. "We are together. And we are safe. That is only by God's power."

He was awake. Kamia and Lara looked back at the man that approached them. His hair disheveled and his face had the distinct imprint of palm fronds on his cheek. He sat down next to Kamia. "It's been a long time since I trusted in God, but this event, from the moment I got the call that I had a daughter, has opened my eyes. He is good, Kamia. He brought you to me."

Lara's eyes filled with tears, and she turned away.

"But we are stranded on—"

"And we have fresh water, good meat, and each other. God has a purpose. I don't know what it is, but He has one. That you can take to the bank."

"Maybe God can help you make a better shelter?" Kamia smiled, and Lara loved that sarcastically sweet way about her.

Boss chuckled. "Hasn't blown over yet."

Kamia covered her mouth. Boss had been listening to their entire conversation.

"No. Not yet."

"Maybe you can help me reinforce it? It would be great if I didn't have to lose another night's sleep staying up to protect you girls."

"I will help strengthen it."

Lara couldn't help but think God knew what He was doing when He stranded them on that island. Once they were back in California, life would run at a much quicker pace. There would be no time to get to know the girl. And seeing who she was on this island — a capable, strong, hardworking survivor would give Boss a new respect for her.

B oss watched in awe as Kamia reinforced the shelter with cross bars all around to keep it sturdy.

"Grab more sand," she called. "We'll pack it around the bottom."

Boss did not hesitate, grabbing the half of Lara's suitcase that was empty and a coconut shell to dig with, he heaped piles of sand into it and he and Lara heaved it back to where Kamia was fortifying their temporary home.

Lara grabbed the other side of the suitcase and helped him tug the heavy sand to the shelter. Boss watched her in wonder. He'd never thought the girl could be so resourceful and strong. His admiration was growing for her by leaps and bounds. And the smell of her sweet sweat as it cascaded down her arms created a tremendous feeling inside of him. A growing desire to get to know her better. Hearing her speak of God and His purpose gave Boss a new sense of direction. He'd spent the last fifteen years pining over a woman he'd once loved, who rejected him for a family who'd never received her back into their home.

As he helped to pack the sand on the bottom of the hut, inside and out, he wondered at the thought of just how perfect God's timing was. Here he was stranded on an island with the woman he'd tried to push away, just because he was attracted to her, and the daughter he had no idea existed. Did God want the three of them to make a connection? Be a family? He wanted that more than anything, and not just because raising a teenage daughter was hard, but because he could see himself loving once again.

"Pack some more in the back," Kamia instructed as she wove vines through the top. "Especially around the posts."

"She runs a tight shift." Boss wiped the sweat from his brow. "I may have to make this girl CEO of my company."

Lara chuckled as she packed more sand around the hut. "Just how many businesses do you own?"

"Ever heard of 'Big Bass?' It's a chain of fishing supply stores."

"Yeah. I've heard of that. There are chains all over the... you own that?"

"That'd be me."

Lara moved inside the shelter with a handful of sand, packing it in any opening. "I thought you worked for Chandler. How did you manage to open a chain of stores? And why do you still work for him if you don't have to?"

"It's a long story." Boss slid the suitcase to the doorway and stepped inside to help her seal the gaps. "Short of it, Chandler was my first investor. Told me if I made good of it, he'd back me."

"So, you feel obligated to stay on with him?"

"Not obligated. Chandler is my friend. He was the only one who took a chance on me. I remain his chauffeur because I respect him. And he respects me. Well, at least until he finds out, I dropped his hundred-million-dollar jet into the middle of the Atlantic."

"You think he's going to be mad?" she asked, her face only inches away from his.

He reached over and pushed a strand of hair away that stuck to her face. He couldn't resist the urge to touch her. Be near to her. Her eyes closed as if she was savoring his touch. He ran his hand down her face.

"Can I kiss you?"

Her eyes opened, and she nodded.

Excitement rushed through him as his lips touched hers. His hands went around Lara's neck, and he pulled her into him, never wanting to let her go. As they fell back into the makeshift bed, he held her close. *I love you.* He hoped his eyes said what his words could not express. He was falling in love with Lara Davies. And this time, heaven help him, he would not push her away. This time, he would let her in.

"Got it packed in there?" Kamia called from outside.

Lara pulled away from him and turned. *Please don't say you're sorry. Please don't say it was all a mistake.* His heart would break if she said those words.

"Almost done in here," Lara called back. With a quick peck on his lips, she gave him a smile that melted his heart. "Thank you," she whispered. "You don't have a pregnant wife, and three kids stashed somewhere, do you?"

"What? No. Of course not."

"Just checking." Lara brushed up against him as she packed the last pile of sand in the corner and left him there alone to wonder what in the world she was talking about.

Leaving the hut, Boss stood back and took in their work. It was good. Sturdy.

"One more thing," Kamia said. "You think we can get the other panel off that wing and use it as a door? It would be much safer than a towel."

"I can do that." Boss rubbed his chin as he examined the wing. "Yeah. Hand me the knife, I can get that side off."

Kamia tossed the open blade to Boss, and he jumped up as it landed at his feet. "Be careful with that thing." He laughed. "You trying to cut me up with that?"

"If we run out of meat, you'll be the next to go." Kamia slapped her legs at her hilariously funny joke.

"You wouldn't want to eat me," he aske. "I only taste good with steak sauce."

Lara turned from them and headed to where the boar's meat hung to dry. "Even with steak sauce, I bet he's bitter."

Kamia laughed, but Boss wondered if maybe Lara still had some hurt feelings over how he'd treated her before. He'd hoped she was just having fun at his expense with her 'bitter' reference. He brushed it off with a chuckle.

Watching Lara as she took down a strip of drying meat, he couldn't seem to take his eyes from her. She turned, noticed his stare, and smiled shyly at him. Like a teenager crushing on the prettiest girl in math class, Boss's face heated. He returned her flirtatious gesture with a smile of his own and added a wink. Holding the meat away from her body, she walked towards him. Before he could warn her, she stepped on a palm frond, and her legs went out from under her. His hand came up to his mouth as he watched her plop down onto her bottom, the meat hanging high in the air.

Her face turned redder than the meat she was holding. "I'm good. No worries."

"Good thing you saved the meat." Kamia took it from her hand and helped her up with the other. "Are you okay, Mames?"

"I'm okay." She wiped off her clothes. "Those things are slippery."

Kamia kicked it away. "They are sharp too. I snapped off all the ends I could find."

Boss watched the two connect as if they'd known each other for a lifetime. He only hoped he and Kamia could get past the playful jabs and become friends. He didn't dare wish to become a father to her. She was steadily on her way to adulthood, and although he hoped one day she would see him as such, he didn't dare get his hopes up.

With his knife in hand, he diligently scraped the remains away from the boar's pelt to use as a protection from the elements. Lara and Kamia each had slices of meat and made their way to the fire to cook the meat. Too proud to admit his stomach was queasy from all the blood and guts, he did his Daniel Boone best to do his part in their survival. Thankfully, they'd carried the inedible parts to the ocean to be food for nearby fish. Kamia had reminded him to keep the predators away from the smell of blood. She was a smart one, that girl.

Soon the aroma of fresh meat wafted through the camp, making his stomach rumble. He set down the pelt and wandered over to the fire.

"Smells delish!" he said.

"This metal piece is working great!" Kamia answered. "Just like a griddle. You got the posts just high enough above the fire so it wouldn't burn the meat."

It took a moment for Boss to recognize that Kamia was complimenting him. "Well, thank you very much, but it was your idea," he answered. "I never would have thought of it on my own."

"Nana always said, use whatever resources you can find to make the best of your surroundings."

The sadness in the girl's eyes was palpable. She missed her mother. Boss sat down next to her. "I'm proud of you, Kamia. And I am proud to know you."

"Thanks." She leaned her head into his shoulder and sobbed.

Boss wrapped his arm around the girl as his own eyes glistened. Kissing the top of her head, he whispered, "It will be okay. I promise."

Lara watched the display with a sad smile on her face. He turned his head into Kamia's soft brown hair and blinked, releasing tears that had been coming for far too long. He was connecting with the rugged, yet sweet girl, and he knew God would heal their broken hearts. In His way, His time, and on His authority, God would heal them.

Lara turned the meat as he, and his daughter bonded. Boss prayed silently, *Thank you, God, for these two. Only you knew my heart could mend.*

"I think it's done," Lara said. "We have fresh coconuts and berries to go with it."

Kamia lifted her head, wiped away her tears, and smiled. "Good. I'm starving."

"Tonight!" Boss stood. "We feast!" He held up a hand as if he'd won a battle.

The girls giggled. "Yes," Lara agreed. "Let's feast."

10

---

*L*ara and Boss sat by the fire and watched the fiery flames climb the night sky. Lara felt as if she was in heaven. Never had she connected to two people like she did these two. Kamia had gone off to the fortified shelter for the night, and it was just the two of them. Inside, Lara's heart was beyond conflict. She wanted to believe Boss was available to her. She wanted to hope he cared about her. If they could be together, she would live on the island forever. Just the three of them. But she couldn't make herself believe. She'd been burned too many times before to give her heart away again.

Looking out at the night sky, Lara couldn't help being in awe of God's creation. There was no doubt in her mind that God was a creative being.

"You think this is the way God planned it? You know, peaceful and quiet. A chance to look out at the stars and see the grandeur He created," Lara asked.

"I think so. It's so easy to see His glory all around us. In Los Angeles, it's hard to even see the stars behind all the smog and pollution. I wonder if I could buy this island."

"Don't get me wrong." She smiled. "I enjoy having fresh running water and flushable toilets. I just feel like I've missed the point of God creating us in the first place. It's so easy to get wrapped up in life and forget the One who made it all possible."

"It sure is amazing." Boss agreed. "I will never forget this island."

"I know. Right?" Lara had made up a hundred excuses to get out of coming, but she was glad she had. She may never want to fly in an airplane again or squat to use the bathroom in the woods, but she would always remember this time. Now, if only someone would find them.

"I just wish I'd have known about Kamia sooner. I feel like so I have lost much time. Time I can't get back." He placed an arm around her shoulder.

"But you are here now. I saw the way she interacted with you. You two will be fine."

"Speaking of fine," Boss said with a chuckle. "That kiss, in the hut, I enjoyed it."

Lara's heart pumped heavily in her chest. "I did, too."

"But afterward, uh, what was that comment about me having three kids and a pregnant wife?"

Lara fell back onto the sand and laughed. "I'm sorry. It was just a joke."

Boss leaned back next to her and pointed her face to his. "What happened?"

Lara stared into his eyes through the darkness and wished she could crawl inside and be safe forever. She felt vulnerable telling him just how naïve she was to fall for that guy's sweet talk. And even more vulnerable opening up to him.

Closing her arms around her chest, she spoke. "I met this guy in Vegas a long time ago. You know, on that trip with Chloe."

Boss chuckled. "Yeah, that's where she met Max. I hear some wild times were had."

"Yeah, so I hear. Too bad I can't remember any of it. Anyway, the guy was from Texas. We exchanged numbers on the plane back and ended up talking to each other. A lot. Like every day. I thought he liked me." Lara rubbed her arms. "I was so stupid to think he could fall for someone like me." She hated herself for falling for the man's charm. "Turned out he was married."

Boss turned to her. "With three kids?" He wiped the tears that flowed freely from her eyes.

"And a pregnant wife." She tried to sound casual, but it still stung.

"And why does that make you stupid?"

"Because ... it just does."

"That's not a good answer. Tell me, why does believing another person has honest intentions make you stupid? In my eyes, it makes *them* stupid." Boss kissed her nose gently as another tear fell. "Makes me stupid." He kissed the tear away from her cheek. "Makes any man who ever had the chance to be in your life, stupid." His lips covered hers with a gentle kiss. "I don't want to be stupid anymore."

With her heart overwhelmed with love, she leaned up and returned his kiss. Only this was not the peck they shared earlier. It was so much more. Her brain tingled with energy. This is the one. Callan Hemsworth, he's the one. When he removed his warm lips from hers, she felt lost. She wanted him to kiss her again. And again. And again.

"Do you accept my apology?" he asked.

"I don't know about that. Maybe one more kiss to seal the deal?"

"Deal." He leaned in and kissed her again. All the hurt and pain from the past released from inside her and she felt God's grace swell up in her chest. Finally, the man she'd waited so long for.

"How about now?" he said as his lips left hers.

"I forgive you," she whispered.

"Good. Let's go try out that new shelter. I promise to keep my hands to myself." He stood holding a hand out to help her up.

"And your lips, too?"

"My lips, too. For now."

"Maybe just one more before we go in?"

Boss wrapped her in his arms. "My pleasure, Madam." He kissed her again.

When they pulled the steel door from the entrance, Kamia was spread out in the middle of the makeshift bed. Lara thanked God. She and Boss would have to climb in on either side of Kamia and would have no further contact until morning. That was a good thing. She had no intention of sharing anything more than a kiss with anyone but a husband.

As she crawled in on one side of Kamia and cuddled in, a silly thought came to mind. If they were stranded on the island long term and decided to marry, who would perform the ceremony? Kamia? She stifled a giggle and turned to face the hut. That wouldn't happen.

"What's so funny?" Boss whispered across from Kamia.

"Nothing," she answered. "Just a silly thought. Good night, Callan."

"Good night. Sweet dreams."

"Oh, cut it out already," Kamia said. "You two lovebirds are keeping me awake."

Lara giggled. "Sorry."

"Mames?" Kamia asked with a yawn.

"Yes, sweetie."

"I've thought it over. I would like you to teach me how to read and write."

Boss sat up. "Wait. What? You don't know how to read and write? You must have gone to school? How is that possible?"

"It's possible," Kamia said and rolled over.

"I'd be happy to teach you how to read and write, Kamia."

Lara smiled. What had she gotten herself into? A ready-made family, and for some reason, she didn't mind it at all.

Sometime later, there was a rustling sound outside. Lara sat up to listen. Kamia sat up, too.

"What is that?" Lara asked.

Kamia jumped up, startling Boss and kicked over the metal door. "Ouch!" she yelled as the wing part clamored to the ground. "That thing is heavy."

"What's going on?" Boss asked, but Kamia was already out the door.

"We heard something. You better go check."

Boss jumped up and followed Kamia out. Lara followed behind.

Kamia stood like a brave warrior at the neck of the jungle with her spear in hand. "Yah!" Kamia yelled. "Get out of here if you don't want to be tomorrow's dinner!"

Pigs squealed off in every direction.

"That'll learn 'em." Boss chuckled. "Maybe we should put that meat in the hut with us?"

Kamia looked out to the east. "Sun is rising. I'll get a fire started."

"Nothing like sleeping in," Boss grumbled and went back into the shelter.

Stretching her limbs, Lara made her way towards Kamia who was already getting the fire started. "I actually feel refreshed. It seemed like I was only asleep for a minute."

"Your snoring says otherwise." Kamia threw some more kindling on the fire.

"I don't snore."

"If you say so. We better hunt up some more wood for the fire. Probably should get back down to the waterfall, too. We could all use something to drink."

"Yeah. Okay. Maybe Boss and I can go while you get the meat roasting."

"Think you two can make it without getting hurt?"

Lara smiled. "I think we can. We've made a bit of a trail through the jungle to follow."

"Sounds like a plan. I'll grab some fresh coconuts and have something ready when you get back."

"Did I hear someone mention a trail hike?" Boss said as he sauntered out of the hut. "I'm game."

"Sun will be up soon. Give it about twenty minutes, and you will have full light to see by," Kamia answered.

"Yes, Ma'am. Until then, I'll just enjoy a nice cup of coffee by the fire."

"Oh, how I wish I could have a cup of coffee right about now." Lara breathed in deep as if she was savoring the rich aroma of a fresh-brewed Colombian coffee. "With a dab of cream and sugar."

"Ever drank dandelion coffee?" Kamia asked, spoiling the moment.

"No!" Lara and Boss said in unison.

Kamia shrugged. "Suit yourself. It's good stuff."

"I think I can wait until we get back to civilization," Boss answered, throwing sticks on the fire. "I wonder if I could swim out to the jet and find your duffle bag?"

"Maybe if you had an oxygen tank," Lara said. "I bet it's sunken pretty deep."

Boss didn't think it was too deep in the water. Upon impact, the Bombardier slowed considerably. Still, it was probably not a good idea to put himself in danger. They were all safe for now. If something happened to him, who would be there to take care of them? Who was he kidding? Kamia was more beneficial to the group than anyone. Still, if he wanted to see her grow up, he'd better play it safe. And Lara

...

Just as Kamia had said, twenty minutes later, the sun reached almost mid sky. Plenty of light to see by. She was quite a remarkable young lady.

"Guess we should head out," Boss said. "I'll grab our water carrier."

"Who'd have thought a suitcase would come to so much use?" Lara followed him as they headed into the jungle. Boss grabbed her hand, dragging the empty half-a-suitcase behind him with the other. The silence between them was comfortable. The feeling of love, over-whelming.

"You didn't know Kamia had no education?" Lara asked.

"No. You know more about her than I do. She doesn't seem to want to tell me anything."

"I promised her I would teach her. If it's okay with you."

Boss had the money to hire the finest of tutors, yet he would trust no one more with the education of his daughter than the woman walking next to him. Still, he teased, "What's your qualifications?"

"Does beauty school count? Besides that, I have a high school diploma."

"Perfect. And if she decides she wants to pursue a career in hair, you can get her a scholarship through your salon."

"Callan Hemsworth!" she dropped his hand. "You can afford to pay for her to do anything she wants."

"I know." He chuckled. "I was just teasing. My offer still stands though." He pulled her hand back into his.

"What offer?"

"To help get your salon going. I'll even buy it for you if you like."

"You can't just go around throwing money into a salon you know nothing about. That's not how you made your money, I'm sure."

"It's a good investment. Not to mention a tax writeoff. I applaud your generosity in giving low-income kids a way to gain successful employment. I would love to be a part of that." He stopped. Maybe he'd overstepped. "If you'll let me."

"I'll think about it. I'm not sure what Chloe's intentions are yet. She says she wants to sell it, but then again, she also said she was going to give the baby up for adoption if it didn't stop sitting on her bladder."

"Hormones, huh?"

"Yup. We'll see how it goes, but thank you for the offer. I appreciate it."

He wanted to offer her so much more. She already held his heart. He was willing to give her anything she wanted as long as she never let him go.

As they kept up the pace to the watering hole, the trail grew narrower, and they could not walk side by side. Lara fell in behind him and the suitcase he dragged on the ground.

"Let's see how much water we can get back without it spill—"

Lara suddenly screamed. Boss spun around just in time to see her body jump back through the air as a snake lunged and grabbed onto her lower leg. She fell backward onto the hard ground with a thump. The snake attached itself between her knee and ankle as it tried to get its venom inside of her. Scrambling for his knife, Boss rummaged through his pockets. It was nowhere.

"Get it off me!" she screamed. "Get it off me!"

"Watch your head!" he yelled as he swung the empty suitcase part through the air, slamming it into her kneecap and the head of the snake at the same time. The snake released its hold on her and flew through the air as Lara grabbed at her leg. Tiny specks of blood peeked through the skin.

"Are you okay?" he asked, bending down to inspect the damage.

"I think you broke my kneecap."

Boss couldn't help but laugh. "I meant to hit the snake."

Lara let out something between a laugh and a cry. "Get me out of here, please."

At least she hadn't lost her sense of humor. Boss held a hand out to help her up. She reached out, and he lifted her to her feet.

"I can't feel my leg," she cried as she tried to stand. "It's all numb and tingly."

Boss turned away from her and bent down on his knees. "Can you get your arms around my shoulders?"

Her hands came to his back, and she pulled on her shirt. "I can't reach."

"A little farther," he coaxed as he leaned back as much as he could.

He placed his hand as far back as he could without falling, and she managed to get hers into his.

"Okay, I'm going to lift. Ready?"

"Hurry, please," she cried. "Before that guy's family comes for revenge."

He pulled her up onto his back. With a wobble, he stood and made his way back to camp. "I don't think that guy will slither home anytime soon." He chuckled and headed back toward camp.

"What about the suitcase?" she asked.

"I'll come back for it."

"What if I am permanently damaged? I mean, what if I have to limp through the rest of my life?"

"You won't be." He patted her good leg. "At least not from the snakebite."

Lara slapped his back. "I can't believe you hit me!" She giggled so hard he thought she would fall off his back. "What a way to start a relationship."

Boss stopped walking.

"What?" Lara asked.

"Are we in a relationship?"

"I... well, I mean... is that what you want?"

"I do." He continued his trek.

"Then, I guess we are."

"I like it."

"Just don't go beating me up anymore."

"As long as you don't let any more snakes attach themselves to your leg, I'll be the perfect gentleman."

As they made it to the clearing, the smell of breakfast wafted through the air. Even with the woman on his back, he felt as light as a feather. He'd carry her to the ends of the earth if that were what it took to keep her around.

Kamia was cutting meat from a coconut as he approached her. Without looking up into their direction, she said. "That was quick. I found some—" Her head lifted and her brows knit. "Boss, what happened? What did you do to her?"

"He cracked me over the knee with the suitcase."

Boss kneeled by the fire to let Lara down carefully. "I got the snake off ya, didn't I?"

"You got bit by a snake?" Kamia rushed over to her. "Man, you are so bruised up." She looked at Boss. "You hit her with the suitcase?"

Boss busted out into uncontrollable laughter. With Kamia staring at him, one hand on her hip, the knife in the other, he tried to contain his amusement and sat down next to Lara. "She was... the snake grabbed onto... all I had was the suitcase... you had the knife..." Tears streamed down his face. "I meant to hit the snake!"

"Did you get it?" Kamia stared back and forth between the two of them.

"He did." Lara laughed. "It went flying through the jungle."

"We are going to need to wrap that up." Kamia seemed to be the only person not amused by the situation.

"It's numb. I can't feel a thing." Lara's face grew as serious as Kamia's.

"It will go away. Well, at least the snake venom will. Remember, I told you, it's not very dangerous to adults? Why did it attack you?"

Lara looked at Boss. "I think maybe he woke it up by dragging that case behind him... and then I aggravated it more by stepping on it. It all happened so fast. I felt something squishy underneath my shoe, and before I could react, it just popped up and went to town on my leg."

"He felt threatened," she agreed. "Probably not many people have been on the island. There are no trails or signs of human life. We have to be the first in a long time. We are disrupting their environment."

"Yeah, and killing off their pig population for meat probably doesn't give them a warm and fuzzy feeling toward us." Boss pulled off his shirt, leaving him with nothing but a tank underneath. Grabbing the knife, he tore his shirt into shreds and began wrapping Lara's leg. "I truly am sorry."

He took a breath to contain another bout of hysteria. He couldn't help it. From the moment he saw Lara lying on the ground with a snake attached to her leg, he'd gone on high alert, but watching that thing fly through the air was comical to him. A brown tree snake bite was not fatal to adults. He knew that. But the look on her face — priceless.

"How long before I can feel my leg?" Lara watched as Boss wrapped his shirt shreds tightly around her leg.

"From the bite or the hit?" Kamia asked.

"Both."

"Maybe by tomorrow you will feel better from the bite. That bruise will take much longer to heal."

Suddenly, Boss's thoughts turned serious. He'd put the woman through so much since he'd laid eyes on her. With the initial snub after their first date, he'd hurt her. They'd had such a connection. And then crashing into the ocean and almost drowning her, well that, although out of his hands, was strike two. With this last incident, he should sit in the dugout watching the game play out. But that wasn't the case, Lara was still there. And somehow, he was still up to bat. Physically, she had no choice. She was stuck with him. But emotionally, she hadn't checked out, and that told him a lot about her.

Boss stood. "I better go get the suitcase and fill it with water. We will need it soon."

"You can't carry that back all by yourself," Lara said.

"I'll manage. If I can carry a load on my back that weighs —"

"Hey!" Lara called. "Watch it."

"What? I was talking about my days in the Navy."

"Good save." Lara laughed. "But as I said before, you are not a young buck anymore."

"Says you." He grabbed a spear. "Hey, Kamia. How does brown tree snake taste?"

"Don't you dare, Callan Hemsworth!" Lara cried. "I never want to see another tree snake again, ever."

Boss chuckled as he made his way into the jungle. He hated snakes, probably more than she did. A small fear crept over him as he made his way back to the spot where they'd left the suitcase. All the while, he brushed his spear across the ground far ahead of him just in case there was something underneath waiting to lunge at him. All the while another fear hid in the back of his mind. When would the rescuers find them? He doubted a search party was even looking yet. He counted the days in his head. With the flight there, three days of waiting for test results and three more spent on the island, they were just nearing the week mark he told Chandler he'd take.

Then again, Chandler would be another week with his wife and child with nothing but his cell phone. Dena had convinced him to leave all work behind and that included his laptop. He knew Chandler was corresponding with his billion-dollar company through his phone when he could get away with it. The man had come a long way from being married to his business to enjoying the family life, but old habits die hard. It mattered little. Both his and Lara's cell phones were sunk to the bottom of the ocean floor. Even if they had them, there would be no signal to call for help. Their best chance was to keep the fire lit and hope for rescue.

He continued to follow the trail as thoughts rummaged through his brain. There was just so much to do when he got back. Check on Will, his chain manager, and arranging the meeting for the new store opening in Anaheim, were his two biggest items. And Kamia. He still had to figure out how to fit her into his small condo. No way would that happen. He'd have to sell the condo and move. He moved house shopping to the top of his list. Maybe Lara would help him find the perfect house, one he hoped she'd one day accompany them in. The thought of a second marriage scared him more than the wildlife he trudged through. Doubts lingered in his mind. He loved Lara, but could he marry again?

Twigs snapping off in the distance brought him back to reality. Keep your head in the game, kid. We have to get off this island before you go having wild dreams of marriage and family. Glancing around, he saw an oversized boar rushing back into a thicket. He continued his trek, focusing on the ground and what might jump out at him.

The suitcase was right where they left it. Poking it with his spear, Boss nudged it a bit to make sure nothing would pop out at him from underneath. When nothing happened, he lifted it from the ground and headed to the waterfall to fill it. Lara was right. He was not a spring chicken anymore. It would be heavy, but he would make it. For her, he would do just about anything.

The fresh water was only a couple yards away. They had almost made it there when they'd gotten waylaid by the snake. He chuckled again at the thought.

Once there, he sunk the suitcase into the water and watched it fill. Lifting it back up, he placed it on the side of the bank and sat a bit to rest. The way back would be longer, and the load heavier. Wiping his brow on his shirt, he bent down and took in the freshwater. Refreshed and ready, he lifted his burden and headed back to the camp. Holding the suitcase with both hands, Boss had no choice but to leave his spear behind. He said a small prayer for God to be his protector as he lugged the heavy item back to camp.

11

*D*ark clouds covered the sky, a sure sign of a storm heading their way. It had only been hours, and already her leg was getting feeling back into it. Her knee still throbbed from Boss bashing it in, but with a limp, she managed to walk on it with little trouble. Sure, it was nothing but bruising. She thought it fun to exaggerate her stride just to stop Boss's incessant laughing at that dumb old snake attacking her. It helped little though, because each time he saw her limp, that familiar guffaw came from deep within his belly. She could do nothing but shake her head.

"It's going to rain," Lara said. "Where's Boss?"

"I'm here," Boss said, coming into the clearing lugging the heavy water-filled suitcase. Lara leaned up and looked to see that most of the water had splashed out and spilled all over his clothes.

"Looks like you spilled a little."

"A bit. It looks like it's going to rain, anyway. I could have waited and let the storm do the job." He set the suitcase down. His arms bulged, showing he was still in great shape. Lara admired his strength.

Kamia looked up at the sky and then back to them. "It's going to be a bad one. Hurry. Grab more sand. Clothes. Rocks. Everything you can to weigh down the hut."

Boss and Lara immediately complied. Kamia and Boss dragged boulders to fortify the sides inside and out, making it more durable and less apt to fly away. Together they piled sand up against the hut on all sides until it almost reached the top. They piled the excess clothes and boar's hide on top of the hut to keep out as much rain as possible.

"More sand. Cover the clothes on the top. Just enough to keep them from blowing away. Too much and it will cave in on us."

Before they finished, the shelter looked more like a sand igloo than a hut made from wood and palm fronds.

"The sand will weigh it down," Kamia said. "The more we pack it, the less that will wash away from the rain."

And sure enough, within the hour, the rain was pouring down on them. There was not even a light sprinkle before the downpour came, forcing them into the shelter.

Once they placed the metal piece over the door opening, darkness hit Lara like the black plague.

"Ouch," Kamia said. "Step on your own feet."

"Sorry," Boss answered. "Didn't see you there."

The rain came down in sheets so hard they had to stop talking. It was no use trying. The sound of the storm drowned out all efforts to hear each other. They hadn't gotten the chance to put out the fire or grab the food, but that didn't matter now. The fire was surely out and the food supply soaked.

The wind whistled around them, tugging at the sides of the shelter, yet not a drop had made its way inside. They sat in silence staring into the darkness, Lara prayed for God's protection. If their only protection failed them, they would not survive in the elements. A clap of thunder rang out, proving her point, and Lara grabbed for Boss. His hand came firmly around hers and held it tight. *God help us!*

Lara laid her head on his shoulder and closed her eyes. The air was unnaturally stale and humid. She tried to go to sleep like she did when she was a kid and her parents got the family together for the long drive to Oregon to visit relatives. The hum of the car would put her to sleep just as the rain made her feel now. The only difference was the claps of thunder ringing out so loudly it made her insides quake. The sky rumbled again, and Boss squeezed her hand tighter.

Kamia relaxed with her head in Lara's lap, sound asleep. How the girl could sleep through all the racket was beyond her.

After over an hour of persistent pounding, the rain was not dying down. "When is it going to stop?"

The sand was starting to wear away because droplets of water began making its way to the inside. The humidity level had risen a million percent, and Lara's body felt sticky and cold. She struggled just to take a breath.

"It's the beginning of typhoon season. If we are lucky, this dumb shack won't cave in on us," Kamia yelled back as she sat up and yawned.

"Don't worry. We'll be fine," Boss said, but something told Lara he was just as worried.

"Soon, I hope," Lara laid back and tried to relax. The wind whistled outside as the shelter shook. It wouldn't be long before it flew right up over them, leaving them exposed. Off in the distance, the sound of branches breaking off and landing on the ground made her shiver. The wind rose so high against the hut. Lara was convinced that at any moment it would collapse on top of them. Lara grabbed back onto Boss's arm and held it tight.

He chuckled. "It's just a little rain."

"A little? I feel like the three little pigs in their house of straw!"

Boss let out a hearty laugh at that. Lara found nothing funny about it. Still, she gave a nervous laugh.

Kamia grew closer. "Tell me a story. When I used to get scared, my mom would read to me."

It was an excellent idea. Something to take their minds off the storm. Lara thought of a story. One that told of bravery she didn't feel. With the rain pouring down on them, only one story came to mind. "Ever hear of Jonah?" She moved closer to Kamia so she wouldn't have to yell.

"Tell me again," Kamia said.

The two of them cuddled together. Boss wrapped the towel around them and leaned back.

"Jonah was a prophet of Israel…" She continued the story.

By the time she finished, the rain was still coming down, but it had slowed. At least the wind wasn't blowing as hard as it had been. She couldn't help but think that God had protected them as He did with Jonah when he got swallowed by the fish. There was no other reason they were still alive and safely huddled together under the warmth and safety of the shelter.

"Why didn't Jonah want the others to be saved?"

Lara shifted. "The Israelites were God's chosen people. I think Jonah had a 'me' complex. Like he was better than the Ninevites."

"I guess so. It's still pretty messed up."

"Yeah. But that story wasn't supposed to tell us so much of Jonah's selfishness than God's love."

"I guess." Kamia pulled away a bit. "I think it's almost over."

"How long do they normally last?" Lara asked.

"Could be a couple of days or only a day," Boss chimed in.

"Great!" It had only been a couple of hours, and already she was ready to get out of the stale, sticky air of the shack.

"But that's for a typhoon," Kamia answered. "I think this is just a disturbance. If it were a full-blown typhoon, this little hut would be a pile of rubbish by now. We'd be running through the pouring rain, dodging lightning bolts."

"Great mental picture. Thanks," Lara said.

"You're welcome. I think it will be over soon."

"Wanna play a game?" Kamia asked.

"Sure," Boss answered. "How about the quiet game?"

"What's that?" Kamia leaned around Lara and crinkled her nose at her father.

"It's a game we played as kids when our mother wanted us to be quiet. Everyone stops talking and we see who can out-silence the rest."

"That's no fun," Kamia said.

"How about *I Spy*?" Lara suggested.

"Yeah, right," Boss said. "How many things can you spy in this ramshackle? Oh yeah, I spy something wet."

Kamia and Lara laughed. "Okay," Lara gave in. "Quiet game it is."

Lara laid down, and the others followed suit. She closed her eyes and tried to fall asleep. If the hut was going to drift away in the pouring rain, there was nothing she or anyone else could do. And the sound of the rain drumming on the roof made her tired eyes droop. Just for a little bit, she thought.

Sometime later, a steady stream of water poured into the hut and down onto Lara's face. Sitting up, she grabbed the towel and wiped her face. Boss and Kamia were still fast asleep. The rain outside dropped steadily onto the roof. Streams of water fell from all directions. The whistling of the wind had died down to a slower pace. She didn't know how long it had been, but she had a feeling it was almost over.

"You okay?" Boss asked, sitting up next to her.

"Yeah, I'm fine. Just a little wet." Lara patted the wet spots on her leg.

"I won." Kamia popped up.

"You won what?" Boss raised his brow.

"The quiet game. You guys are a tough crowd to beat." Kamia sat up and wiped at her eyes. Yawning, she said, "So what did I win?"

"How about a kick in the pants?" Boss said.

Kamia wrinkled her nose at him. "You're no fun."

"You think it's safe to go outside yet?" Lara asked no one in particular.

"It sounds like it's just about over and I'm starving," Kamia said. "Do we have any berries left out there?"

"I'll go see what I can find." Boss got to his knees. "There's a bush just outside the woods."

"Maybe you should stay for a little longer," Lara said. "It's got to let up soon."

"It could go all day," Kamia answered. "I can go. I'm used to the weather."

"I'll go," Boss insisted. "Already got my shoes on. Bet I can find a couple of coconuts on the ground as well."

"Use your belt. You can shimmy up a tree."

Boss chuckled. "Yeah, right. I'll leave the tree shimmying to you. Be back soon." Boss kicked open the door and a stream of water flooded in. Along with it came a cool breeze. It felt good to breathe fresh air again.

"So much for keeping somewhat dry." Lara stood to dodge the river that flowed in around her. "Guess it couldn't be helped."

Boss shrugged. "Sorry about that. I'm out to find food."

Boss lifted the door to close it again and stop the rest of the flooding.

"Leave it open," Lara said. "If we have to be soaked to the bone, at least we can air out the place, too."

Nodding, Boss flopped it back onto the wet sand.

Boss grabbed one of the spears that sat in a puddle by the now drenched fire and headed off to the jungle. The wind had died down considerably, but was still enough to keep Boss's clothes whipping through the air. Making it to the berry bush he'd spotted, he found it wiped clean. On the ground below, purple wild berries floated in the puddles of water. They were no longer edible. They took refuge in a mixture of mud and leaves. Sighing, he looked into the jungle. He'd have to make his way further in if they wanted to eat.

As his eyes adjusted to the darkness, he tried to keep his pace quiet and stay on the trail they'd worn through the jungle. He was sure all the animals were in hiding. He didn't worry too much about being pursued by a predator of any kind. Still, he kept his spear close just in case. He followed the path, looking fiercely for something to eat. Slipping once or twice, he managed to catch himself before landing in the mud. All the while, his thoughts were on the girls. He needed to find something quick and get back to them. The worst of it was over, but all he could think about was that shamble of a hut caving in on them.

Off in the distance, a hint of light shone on a couple of coconuts that lay on the ground, but they were off the path. Boss didn't want to go into the denser parts if he didn't have to. He kept walking. There was another berry bush ahead. He couldn't see it yet, but remembered they'd picked from it before. He just hoped it was protected from the strong winds by the surrounding trees. Rain misted around him, much of it caught in the greenery above. With all the heavy rains, it was no wonder the place grew plush with vegetation. There was no one there to bother it, and the rains kept it hearty and healthy.

Before he knew it, he had reached the end where Kamia and Lara had squeezed through the tiny entry between the trees to get to the water. He chuckled inwardly at the thought of Lara being almost attacked by a boonie pig and squeezing her body through to get away. He peeked through and saw that the water had risen considerably. There would be nothing there for them to eat.

Water poured droplets into the water basin. It was a beautiful sight. The sun peeked through the clouds just enough to remind the island that it was still there and would soon come out to dry them off.

Up on the other side, he saw a bush. It was ripe with fruit, undamaged by the winds. He made his way around the bend and over to it. Picking all he could and holding them in his shirt like he did when he was a kid catching bullfrogs, he filled it up with as many as he could carry.

When he'd picked the bush almost clean, he headed back. Lara and Kamia would be grateful for his catch. Poking the ground as he went, he made his way back down the path with his prize, eating a couple here and there as he went. Back at the spot where he'd seen the coconuts on the ground, he grabbed them. Who knew how long it would be before the rain completely stopped, and they could catch some fish. Of course, if he'd have let Kamia come, she'd have speared some fish and have them grilling by now. Not in this rain. Even Kamia couldn't successfully start a fire until the rain stopped and the wood dried.

Taking small steps out onto the slick jungle floor, Boss was careful to not step on anything that might be sleeping. When he reached the coconuts, he realized he could not carry them back with one hand holding up his shirt full of berries and the other holding a spear. Food or safety? It was a toss-up. Dropping the spear on the jungle floor, Boss decided the food was a priority. Besides, he wasn't far away now.

Juggling one coconut in his arm and the other in his free hand, he headed back for the trail. As he stepped onto the path, his foot slipped out from under him and he fell to the ground. Before he had time to let out a hearty yell, the world went dark.

"What's taking him so long?" Kamia asked. "He's been gone for hours."

Lara was sure it hadn't been hours, but one at least. Way too much time for him to be gone. She worried as well. A clap of thunder sounded, reminding them that the storm was not over. Lara rubbed at her arms. She just couldn't get used to those loud booms. Back home, she would run inside, but here, their inside was a flooded mess of sand and water.

"Should we go out and look for him?" Lara asked.

"Maybe he's feasting on berries, while we sit here starving to death," she answered.

"You think?"

"I don't know. You know him better than me. I just met him."

"He's your father."

"Not until a week ago."

"Okay. We'll give him another fifteen minutes, and then we'll go looking for him," Lara said, not sure how they would decide when fifteen minutes were up. They'd have to narrow it down to the nearest second.

The slowing rhythm of the rain made Lara feel much better. She wasn't excited about going out into the jungle in the pouring rain looking for a man who was probably trying to climb a tree to bring back fresh coconuts for them. That thought scared her even more. As good of shape Boss was in, she didn't think he took her seriously when she mentioned the fact that he wasn't as young as he thought he was.

Waiting, she counted off the seconds in her head. It wouldn't do to scare Kamia into thinking something might be wrong. The girl had been through too much already.

"Let's go," Kamia said before Lara could suggest it. "I'm getting worried."

"Okay, sure." Lara pretended she wasn't afraid. "The rain has slowed. We can help him gather coconuts."

Kamia grabbed a spear and handed one to Lara. As they trudged through the wet sand, the water puddled, making soft holes under their feet. The trees were weighed heavy with rain. Soft sprinkles fell on them, but it felt good. Lara cast her gaze into the sky. The clouds were dissipating, and the sun was making its presence known.

Kamia looked up, too. "It's going to be a hot one tomorrow. Always is after a good storm."

"At least we survived. Let's go help Boss with the food. I bet he's got a whole bunch of good stuff."

Staying on the trail, they looked for Boss. She'd thought he was going to hit that one berry bush sitting at the edge of the jungle, but after finding it bare, she realized he'd had to go in. The fresh tread marks proved her theory. Neither of them wore a size thirteen shoe. They could only be his, and they were leading right down the path, and all going one direction. There were no return prints. He was still in there somewhere.

They walked a good distance before Kamia spoke. "What's that?" She pointed off ahead of them.

"What? Where?"

"Over there, on the ground. It looks like a lump of… black and blue."

As soon as she caught what Kamia was speaking of, she knew what it was. Boss. He'd been wearing the Raider jersey he stole back from her when he left. The two of them had fought over it the night before. "It looks like a dress on you," he'd joked.

"I like it. It's comfy."

Obviously, he'd won the battle because he was wearing it. And there he was lying on the ground, face up, unmoving.

Lara took off in a half jog, half limp, and Kamia followed behind. The sound of their feet crunched across the ground as they made their way to Boss.

"Is he okay?" Fear filled Kamia's voice.

Lara looked him over. Bright red blood drizzled from the side of his head and onto a boulder next to it. His clothes were soaked with water, sticking to his brawny body. His face held a look of serenity. Was he dreaming he was back home again?

"He's lost a lot of blood." The steady rise and fall of his chest indicated he was not dead but only passed out. Pulling off her shirt, she ripped it to shreds. She was naked, besides her bra and shorts, but modesty was not important at that moment. Stopping the bleeding on Boss's head wound was the only thing that mattered.

Lara wadded up her shirt and held it to his wound. Dried blood stuck stiffly to his hair. How long had he been here? "We have to get him back to camp."

"There's no way we can carry him," Kamia said what she was thinking. "He's got to weigh a ton."

"We'll have to stay with him until he wakes." Lara lifted his head gently, seeing the moss and leaves that stuck to the back of his neck and shoulders.

"Maybe we should at least get him on the trail?" Kamia asked, her voice a whisper.

The thought of what kind of predator the scent of his blood would attract made Lara readily agree. "Grab his legs. I'll get his shoulders."

Kamia did as Lara told her. For the first time since they met, the young girl was not calling the shots. Lara looked up and saw a fear that matched her own on the girl's face. But she could not let hers show. She knew nothing about first aid past the class she'd taken in high school. And that was not much.

Dragging him the few feet onto the trail, Lara sighed. "He's so heavy," she said.

"Like a ton of soaking wet bricks."

They got him going sideways on the trail, and Lara sat in the mud, lifting his head onto her lap. Keeping continuous pressure on his wound, she did her best to keep his head raised above his body. She wasn't sure why, or if that was even a thing, but it seemed like the right thing to do, and she felt better keeping him close to her.

"Can you make it to the water? We will need something to clean his wound," Lara said. "And drink. I'm thirsty. I know he will be too."

Kamia stood. They weren't very far off from the water, so it wouldn't take her long. Grabbing a coconut, Kamia smashed it on a nearby rock, splitting it in two, and took off toward the waterfall.

"Kamia," Lara called.

Kamia turned.

"He's going to be okay. Take your time. Drink some water yourself."

Kamia nodded and kept walking.

"God, please let him be okay." Lara was scared. As tough as she wanted to be for Kamia, Lara feared he would die. There was just so much blood. She said a prayer for him, and for them. God had protected them so far, but it was hard to keep faith when her circumstances seemed so dire.

Moments later, Boss stirred, and his eyes opened. Turning his head to see his surroundings, he had no idea she was there, holding up his bandaged head. Slowly, he put his hands to the ground and tried to sit up.

"Don't move," she breathed. "Kamia has gone to get water."

"What happened?" His eyes veered up to hers, and then he closed them. "That hurts."

"I think you fell. The ground is super slippery. You hit your head on a sharp rock."

"Am I bleeding?"

"Uh, huh."

"Why don't you have a shirt on."

Lara paled. She'd forgotten she'd taken it off. "It's on your wound. I had to stop the bleeding."

"I saw nothing, I swear." He started to laugh but grabbed his head. "Oh, that hurts."

"That's what you get," she teased, so happy he was alive.

"Did the berries survive?"

"Not unless we want a blend of berry juice and mud."

He tried to raise his head again.

"Boss, stop it. I mean it," she chided. "Kamia will be back in a minute, and then we can try to help you up."

"What's she doing, making a sling to carry me in?"

"She's getting water," Lara reminded him.

"Oh, that's right." His eyes opened to small slits. "I'm thirsty."

"Close your eyes until I get a shirt on."

"It's going to be a long walk back if I can't see where I'm going."

"It's going to be a long time in the jungle by yourself if you open your eyes again."

Boss chuckled, making himself cringe in pain.

"That's what you get."

"Right. Eyes closed. Got it."

Lara smiled at his playfulness. He would be just fine. Still, she needed to cover herself, and soon.

Less than ten minutes later, Kamia returned with two coconut bowls full of water. "How's he doing?"

"I'm fine, but Lara won't let me open my eyes," he called.

"Won't what?" Kamia looked to Lara's state of undress. "Oh!"

Kamia came up next to them and set the bowls down. "Here." She pulled up her own shirt, revealing a tank underneath.

"Oh, thank you! The mosquitoes are eating me alive!" Lara said. At least Boss wouldn't have to walk all the way back with his eyes closed.

"I'll hold his head. You put your clothes on." Kamia placed her hand over the covered wound, and Lara stood.

"Yeah. Put your clothes on, girl," Boss said.

"Lucky for you, you're already hurt, or I'd have to smack you," Lara teased as she pulled the shirt around her. Good thing for her, it was one of Boss's oversized tees. She'd never fit into one of Kamia's.

"Lucky me. Can I open my eyes now?"

"Yes," Lara said, letting the shirt drop around her waist. "It's safe."

Boss opened his eyes. "Help me up, please."

"Let's get him sitting," Lara said. "He might be dizzy for a second." She held out her hands and let him use them to pull himself to a sitting position. Kamia held the shirt to his wound as she gently pushed on his shoulders.

Once in a sitting position, Lara passed him a coconut bowl. "Drink up. We need to get back to camp before the snakes come out."

"Or the boars," Kamia said. "I'm sure the smell of blood is thick in the air."

The thought made Lara recoil. "Yes, let's hurry."

"Wait," Kamia said. "Lara, hold the shirt to his head."

Lara did as she was told but looked at the girl questioningly.

"What's she doing now?"

"I don't know. My head is throbbing and swirling right about now."

"Give it a second and the swirling part should go away. The throbbing is another story." Lara was reminded of her aching knee. She hadn't thought about it once in all the drama of thinking Boss would die. At the thought of helping him all the way back to camp, it throbbed as well. *Aren't we a fine mess?*

Soon Kamia was out of sight. The rain had stopped, but still, she worried. The ground was still slippery, and she couldn't deal with another casualty. A few minutes later, Kamia was back with a length of vine in her hand.

"You going to tie me up?" Boss asked. "Is it not bad enough I'm dying here?"

Kamia rolled her eyes. "I'm not going to tie you up."

Kamia unraveled and pulled on the natural rope. "It's strong." She then gently pulled the t-shirt away from his wound.

"Maybe it's not a good idea?" Lara said.

"It's not bleeding anymore. But it may start again." She pushed it gently back to his head. "We can tie it down with this." She held up the twine again.

"Wait," Boss said. "You are going to tie that rope around my head like a mummy"?"

"Just your forehead, silly," Kamia answered. "we can't very well hold you up while Lara's got one hand on your head, can we?"

Before he could object again, she was already wrapping the vine around his head over the t-shirt and back to the front. She wrapped it several more times and then tied it with a knot in the back. "That should do."

Boss mumbled something incoherent and lifted his hands up for help to a standing position.

"What was that?" Kamia asked.

"I said thank you for making me look like Rambo."

Lara covered a giggle. "A very cute Rambo, I must say."

"And clumsy," Kamia added.

Lara wasn't sure Kamia knew who Rambo was, but still, she thought the girl had amazing wit.

"Thanks," Boss mumbled. "See if I try to get you berries ever again."

"You leave the hunting to me, and we'll be just fine."

❧

Boss had a headache the size of North America. The back of his head throbbed and pulsed against the vine Kamia had tied around it. With Lara's limp and his slow pace, it had taken them an hour to make the fifteen-minute walk back to the camp, and now, as he lay on the damp towel by the fire, his stomach rumbled. He didn't dare complain. Kamia was likely off killing something for them to eat.

"The shelter is flooded." Lara sat down beside him. "I pulled out all the clothes and palm leaves to dry out so maybe we can sleep in it tonight."

"It will dry out quickly. The sun is out in full force. Won't take long."

He'd have loved to be more conversational, but with each open of his mouth, his head pounded harder.

As if seeing the pain in his face, Lara said, "Why don't you try to get some sleep. It may help with the pain." Boss closed his eyes and relaxed his head on the makeshift pillow Lara had made for him.

"Can you take this contraption off my head?" He reached up to pull on the vine attached to his forehead.

"Let me help." Lara pulled on the vine, tugging at his wound.

"Careful, would ya. That hurts."

"Sorry." Lara managed to get the thing off his head without too much more pain.

As soon as it was gone, his head felt much better. "Thanks."

Sleepy, he closed his eyes to rest, but just as he was dozing off, a shuffling came from the jungle. He opened his eyes and slowly turned his head. Kamia was back. He kept his eyes opened just enough to see her walking through the jungle with the towel slung over her back in a makeshift backpack. Why hadn't he thought of that when he'd gone out to gather berries? Sitting down beside him, she unfolded the towel and pulled out several good-sized fish and some kind of plant. "What's that?"

"For pain. It's called Lagundi. Once it's boiled, you will drink it every four hours for pain."

"No way, no how. I'll deal." He grabbed at his head again.

"It's very good, Boss. I promise it will ease the pain."

"Can't you just place it on my head?"

Kamia lowered her brows. "Like a hat?"

"Ugh. No! I'm not drinking that."

"Suit yourself. I will boil it in case you change your mind."

Before he could ask how in the world she would boil the stuff, she placed it into a coconut bowl, poured in some water and set the concoction right on the metal skillet. Closing his eyes, he tried to sleep. Does she think she's a Suruhåna?

Living with Isa, he'd learned much about the Chamorro ways.

Although many were of the Catholic religion, they still held to the old superstitions and ways of the ancient Chamorros. Isa had gone to a Suruhåna when she'd come down with a stomach virus. She'd refused to go to the Navy hospital.

"The Suruhåna can cure any ailment," She'd told him. The medicine gurus used all kinds of spiritual prayers and incantations mixed with herbal remedies to heal their people. No offense to the natives, but he didn't believe in that stuff. God was the only healer. Still, many plants on Guam had medicinal uses. Maybe she was right. But if she started chanting over him, he was out of there.

A good fifteen minutes later, his head pounded so hard he couldn't sleep. He sat up and grabbed his head. "Okay, okay, give me some of that stuff. Anything to stop the pain."

"It's cooling. A few more minutes and I will give you a dose." Kamia grinned as if she'd won a huge battle.

He held his throbbing head and watched the Suruhåna stir her mixture. *This stuff better work.* Lara sat next to him, filleting the scaled fish. She kept her head down, struggling to keep a straight face.

"What are you laughing at?" He couldn't help but crack a smile.

"You." She let out the hilarious laugh she'd been holding in. "I keep thinking about you hitting my leg with that suitcase. And now, here you are, looking like Rambo, about to take some herbal medicine for your pain."

"And that is funny to you?"

Her eyes glimmered with laughter, and he couldn't help but smile.

"Yes!" She laughed some more. "Even though the strings are gone, you have an indent all across your forehead."

He found it quite humorous himself, but it hurt too much to laugh. "Is that stuff ready yet?"

"Almost. You know if you would stop barking at me, your head would hurt much less."

Lara burst out in another fit of laughter. Just rolling his eyes brought on another bout of pain.

"I'm sorry," she said, still giggling. "I'm just so happy you are okay." Her face turned serious. "I was really worried for you."

Kamia came over with the coconut bowl full of her crazy medicine concoction. She tipped the bowl to his lips, and he took a sip.

"More," she coaxed, lifting the bowl higher so more would flow into his mouth.

He swallowed a mouthful, then shook his head. "No more. That's enough."

To be truthful, though it was bitter, it didn't taste that bad. Boss laid back and closed his eyes. Within a half an hour, more or less, his headache subsided. Finally, he felt himself falling to sleep.

"Should he sleep with a head wound?" Kamia's voice was like white noise from a fuzzy television channel.

"He'll be fine. We'll wake him every two hours, to be sure he's okay."

13

*I*t had been two more days, another round of pig meat, and plenty of fish later, and not a sign of rescue. They were all tired, and Lara was losing hope. Boss was up and around as if nothing had happened. With some salve, Kamia had made an antibacterial ointment, and his wound was healing nicely. Up until that morning, he'd taken her concoction every four hours, just as she had advised. But this morning, he woke up in a great mood. Lara just wished they could go home. She was tired of worrying and wanted more than anything to soak away the jungle in a hot bath in her own home.

God was on His own time, and He did not plan for them to be stuck out there forever. She just hoped His plan was for them to get rescued soon. Never again would she complain about the things that bothered her back home. Noisy neighbors, rush hour traffic, slow shoppers at the grocer — those were all things she'd gladly endure if God felt the time was right for them to go back to civilization.

"I'll go get water," Kamia said tiredly. The struggle was wearing on her, too.

They'd made a makeshift sled out of braided vines to pull the suit-case through the trail through the jungle. It was much easier, and one person could pull it across the ground rather than trying to carry it. Still, it was grueling work.

"I'll go," Boss volunteered. "It's my turn."

After her run-in with the snake, Lara had been banned from going into the jungle indefinitely, and although she never wanted to go back in again, she felt as if she wasn't pulling her weight. "I can go. My leg feels much better."

"No!" Kamia and Boss said in stereo.

"I'll go." Kamia grabbed the suitcase and headed off into the jungle. "You two find too much danger when you go in there."

"Hey, it was wet!" Boss called. "How was I to know how slippery the ground would be while carrying two coconuts and a shirt full of berries?"

"Yeah. And you ruined my jersey. Those squashed berries will never come out."

"I'll get you a new one. One that fits." Boss winked at Lara, and she blushed.

"I'm going." Kamia slipped on her thin, worn shoes and grabbed a spear.

"Stubborn one," Boss said as he sat down next to Lara.

"Just like her father."

"I have something for you." Boss held out a small ring woven of vines.

"What's that?" She took it.

"It's a promise ring."

"A promise ring?" Her heart fluttered at the gesture. "A promise of what?"

"A promise that we will get off the island soon and I will be able to spoil you properly."

Lara smiled. "A promise, huh?" She slid the ring onto her finger. It fit loosely. "Thank you, but you don't have to spoil me."

"What if I want to?"

His eyes locked onto hers and he leaned in and kissed her.

Breathless, she pulled her head back. "Maybe just a little."

Boss smiled. "Oh, and I promise no more physical damage."

"Not even if I'm being bitten by a snake?"

"Practicing my aim."

"What if a wild boar attacks me?"

"Stab 'em in the neck."

"Thanks." Smiling, she turned away. All the physical pain in the world did not hurt as much as rejection. But she couldn't ask him to love her forever and to take away all her fears. To spend the rest of his life giving her soft kisses. He had to want that. She prayed he did. As much as she wanted to believe he cared, that small nagging in the back of her brain told her she was wrong. Boss was filled with the emotion created by their situation. How could she be sure he was not just feeling overwhelmed? From a little white girl in the ghetto, Lara had always believed that people were essentially good. She'd met many a bully who was only reacting to the pain they'd suffered. Man after man had let her down, and after the last one, her trust was waning. She couldn't take one more jab at her slowly failing heart.

"What are you thinking about?" he asked. "Looks like you are deep in thought."

"Oh, nothing. Just a hot shower and greasy fast food." She wouldn't dare share her insecurities with him. Not now. Maybe never.

"You got that right. If I have to taste one more meal of boar meat or fish, I may go crazy." Boss poked a stick at the fire. "They've got to get here soon. Right?"

"I sure hope so."

"Got any plans after that shower and burger?"

"Get back to work, I guess. I bet Chloe already had her baby."

Boss chuckled. "I bet she did."

"How about you?" she asked

"Besides begging Chandler's forgiveness for wrecking his plane?"

Lara nodded.

"Probably drink a gallon of water, take an hour-long shower, and then set out to buy a bigger house for Kamia and me."

"Why's that?"

"I've got this dinky condo that suited me just fine on my own.

Kamia's not going to want to share a room with a hundred model airplanes. There's not even a bed in there."

"That could be a problem."

His words cut her to the core. Kamia and I. She was acting childish. Of course, he wanted to get a bigger home for Kamia. But what about them? What would happen between the two of them once they got back to civilization? Would they continue to see each other? Would they take it farther? Or would he wrap himself back up in his billionaire life and never call her again? She wanted to believe things had changed between them, but a couple of kisses and a bit of handholding on a deserted island did not constitute a commitment. She swirled her "promise" ring around on her finger. He spoke a lot of words, but what did they all mean? Her heart filled with frustration as she thought through the hard questions until finally, the words burst from her mouth.

"What about us?"

Boss dropped the stick into the fire and watched it catch fire. He turned to her and stared for a long while before speaking. "I want to see you more."

"What if this is all just desperation?" She knew how she felt about him, and it had nothing to do with being stranded on an island. "What if all these feelings are just—"

"Is that what it is for you?"

"No. Not at all. But you—"

"I what?"

"You left. We had a nice time. You kissed me at my door and said you would call me, but you never did." Why couldn't she let it go? "You never called."

Her body trembled. She couldn't take another rejection.

Boss wrapped his arms around her shoulder. "I know. I was scared. I'm sorry."

She lifted her head up. "Scared of what? Me?"

"Yes, you. Lara. You are so sweet and beautiful. Kind. Loving. You remind me of everything I ever loved... and lost. My heart cannot take another break. After Isa, I shut myself off. Believe it or not, you were the first girl I've dated in fifteen years. Ask Chandler or Max. They thought I was crazy. Always trying to set me up with this girl or that. I never took the bait. Not until you. And when I met you and got to know you, I fell in love. That scared me. I mean, a hide in the closet, and never come out, kind of scared."

"I'm sorry, I'm so scary to you." Lara brushed sand on her shoes then shook them off.

"Have you heard a word I said?"

"I heard you. You said you don't want to love and you are afraid of me."

Boss stood. "You are unbelievable."

Lara stood too. "What!" Her voice rose. "You said you couldn't handle another breakup. You are afraid of love. Boss, what do you want me to do about that? I'm not Isa. My goal in life is not to hurt you. I only want—"

Before she could finish, Boss pulled her to him and kissed her until she melted in his arms. When it was over, he stared into her eyes. "Did you miss the part where I said I fell in love?"

Lara's body shook with uncontrollable tremors. "You what?" she rubbed her arms. "I didn't — I guess I missed that part."

"Would you like me to say it again?"

"Please." *Because if you don't, I will never believe I mean more to you than comfort on an island.*

"I fell in love." Still holding her, he rubbed her back. "With you."

Lara turned from him as a new rush of energy passed through her. *God, please don't let him just be saying what I want to hear. He's lonely. He doesn't mean it.* "I better go see what's taking Kamia. She's been gone too long."

"You stay." He kissed her forehead. "I'll go."

"Boss," she called.

He turned.

"I can't do it. I want to, but I can't. I have —" *What? You have what?* "Obligations. Commitments. I can't." Tears streamed down her eyes. *What was she doing?*

"Fine. I can't make you love me, Lara." Boss turned and walked away.

Lara sat on the warm sand. Crying, she prayed. *God, I don't want to be afraid to commit to him. I love him. I just can't get over the feeling that he is suffering from a fifteen-year-old banished lover. I don't want to be his rebound love. I want him to love me fully and completely. I just don't think he can.*

Then say the words. A soft voice spoke to her. She didn't know whether it was The Holy Spirit or her conscience talking. *Say the words. Tell him what he needs to hear. Tell him you love him.*

It was too late. Lara had pushed him away. Those three words were the scariest ever spoken. She'd reserved those for her family and people in her life who had been there for her. The ones she'd do anything for. Anything. But she'd never said them to a man. She did love him. But could she say the words? And after he walked away, hoping to hear her reciprocate, she'd pushed him away. Told him he wasn't important enough to fight for. Obligations? What obligations?

"Found her," Boss came back to camp, pulling the suitcase behind him. He spoke as if nothing was amiss, but he didn't look at her. She'd blown her chance. He was done trying.

A humming sounded high in the sky, and Lara lifted her head to see what it was.

"They found us!" Kamia yelled as she jumped up and down. "Over here! We are over here!"

High in the sky, a helicopter flew closer and closer. Soon it was just over their head.

Boss waved his hands through the air, yelling with Kamia. "Over here! We're over here!"

The wind kicked up as the helicopter hovered above. It was so close; they could see the pilot. He waved at them and smiled. They were rescued. But why did Lara's heart feel stranded?

The helo set down close by, stirring up their belongings. Lara held her hands to her ears to soften the noise. The makeshift hut they'd worked so hard on fell flat to the ground. Clothes flew about as the propellers slowly came to a halt.

A man jumped out of the chopper wearing tan shorts and a matching shirt. "Need some help here?"

"Yes, please!" Kamia shouted.

Boss walked up to the man and shook his hand. Kamia followed behind.

"We are rescued, Mames!" Kamia rushed back and took her hand. "Isn't that great! We don't—" Before she could finish, her face dropped. "I'm scared."

Lara's heart mirrored the girl's words. Soon they would be back in their own homes, doing their own things. She would never again have the opportunity to tell Boss she loved him. Wanted to make a life with him. With Kamia.

"It's okay." She rubbed the girl's back. "It's going to be okay." If only she believed that for herself.

As Boss told the man about the jet losing fuel and how he'd amazingly landed in the water, saving them all, Lara and Kamia stood back and waited.

"Lucky you," the man said, looking around at them. "Got stranded with two beautiful ladies."

Boss waved them forward. "This is my daughter, Kamia." He pulled Kamia closer. "And this is uh—" He looked to Lara, and his voice caught. "Lara."

Just Lara. Not even the friend title he'd introduced her with on Guam. Lara forced a smile and turned. "I'm going to gather our belongings."

"I'll help." Kamia grabbed her hand. "Are you okay?"

Tears stung her eyes, but she would not let the girl see her pain. "I'm great!" she lied. "Tears of joy."

"I am not stupid, Mames. Something is wrong."

Lara grabbed a bunch of clothes and shoved them into a pile. "I'm okay, really. Just a bit overwhelmed. But look, our rescuers are here."

Kamia piled more clothes on the stack. "You will still teach me, right? You promised."

Why had she promised her that? She wanted to teach Kamia. She wanted to be a part of her life, and Boss's too, but maybe it just wasn't in God's plan.

"Yeah, sure. I'd love to, Kamia. Make arrangements with your father."

Kamia stopped her as she went for her towel stuck to the collapsed hut. "He loves you, Mames."

Lara's body tremored. How could she believe he loved her? Because he said it? People will say things when they are desperate. Allowing her anger to rule over her fear, she closed her mind off to it. It was the only way to get through it.

"No, Kamia. He loves your mother."

Kamia went to answer, but Boss and the man from the helicopter walked up, staving off her answer.

"Got everything together?" Boss asked, his words directed to Kamia. His eyes never once veered to Lara's.

"Yeah." Kamia looked to Lara with a sad smile. Even she knew the party was over.

"I have some bags in the copter."

The man went back to the intimidating metal machine and came back with leaf-sized trash bags. One for each of them. Boss grabbed a bag and shoveled in clothes and belongings. At one point, their bodies were so close, Lara could feel the heat emitting from him. He looked up and their eyes connected. Before she could say a word, he looked away.

"Better get that fire out."

"Yeah," she answered and moved to the fire.

Kamia beat her to it. With her feet, she slid mounds of sand onto the smoldering embers. Lara bent down to help. Kamia gave her a look of pity. "What happened between you two?"

"I don't know. I got scared." Why was she consulting a teenager?

"Tell him how you feel."

"I can't. Not now."

The rescue worker walked their way. "Is there anything out there you need to get?" He pointed a thumb into the jungle. "We don't want to disturb the wildlife any more than necessary when we leave."

"No. There's nothing." Lara's voice shook as she answered.

"Are you okay, young lady?" the man asked. He was barely older than her. *Whatever.*

"Yeah. Just tired." She gave the man the same excuse she'd given Kamia. Only Kamia had seen through it. She'd have to do better at hiding her pain.

"Okay, then. I'm sure you guys will need some hydration and a good meal. Let's get you home."

With the fire out and the area cleaned up as best they could, they boarded the chopper. Lara watched as it lifted off and headed away. No longer did her fear of flying bother her. Instead, as she watched the island get smaller and eventually drop out of view, her sadness increased. It had been the most grueling experience of her life, and even though she'd gotten bitten by a snake, scared out of her wits and almost drowned, she had found love. If only...

🐾

After finding out they were being taken back to Guam and not home, Boss was frustrated. He got it. There was no way they were going to fly them all the way back to the states in a chopper.

After each of them getting a full checkup at the Naval hospital, they were deemed healthy. "Never seen someone in such good condition after what you've been through," the doctor said. "Nothing short of a miracle."

The doctor had re-bandaged Boss's head and told him how lucky he was that bacteria hadn't set in an infection. As the man said, it had been a miracle. God had protected him. Them.

But more than the pain that still stung the back of his head, his heart was crushed. She had lied to him. She'd allowed him to kiss her and pour out his heart to her, tell her he loved her and then crushed him all in one sentence. She was no better than Isa.

Had it just been payback? Had she led him on only so she could do to him what he did to her? And to top it all off, he'd offered to pay her fare back, and she'd declined. Two words. "No, thanks." That was all she said to him. Boss slapped his leg in frustration.

It was only him and Kamia, and he would have to make the best of it. The girl was the light of his life. Using the throwaway phone he'd bought on Guam, he sat next to Kamia in the airport and dialed Chandler. Not wanting to recall crashing the man's pride and joy into the ocean, he thought it better he get it over with.

"What's up, Boss?" Chandler called over the squealing toddler in the background. "I hear you wrecked the Bombardier."

He knew. Of course he did. He'd had to have reported them missing for a search helo to come. "I don't know what happened, man. I did all my pre-flight checks. Everything looked good. I was flying out of Guam and next thing I know, I got fuel leaking."

"Hey, man. It's all good. I'm just glad you guys are safe. Insurance will cover it. How's the kid?"

"She's a pretty smart girl. Knew how to hunt and fish. 'Bout saved our lives. Like father, like daughter, eh?"

"Yeah, right. Should have had her fly the plane instead."

Boss chuckled. This was one incident Chandler would never let him forget.

"Yeah. Well, hey, we have a flight out from here soon. I'll see you when we get back."

Boss hung up the phone and watched out the window at a plane taxiing down the field. For a moment, he thought about throwing in the towel on his piloting dream. The incident that happened so long ago rushed back to him in an instant. He'd been an airman in the officer pilot program. He'd trained for hours upon hours on simulator flights before he was qualified to take a plane up with an authorized pilot. On his first flight out, he'd gotten up in the air and almost killed them all. Three passengers on board and he'd flown so low he'd almost clipped a mountainside, endangering him and the rest of them. The warning had sounded for him to bring the plane up, and he froze.

The officer in charge had taken control of the plane, landed it, and kicked him out of the program. And just like that day long ago, he felt that same feeling once again. Only this time it wasn't about flying.

Whatever caused that fuel to leak had been beyond his control. It was about Lara. She'd rejected him, and his heart was as chilled as an icicle.

"What's wrong with you?" Kamia asked, sitting next to him munching on a bag of chips.

"Nothing!" he barked. His brain reasoned with him. It was not her fault. "Just tired, I guess."

"Yeah, me too." She popped a chip in her mouth. "Are there pigs in California?"

Boss looked at her strangely. "Of course, there are. Why?"

"I don't know. I'm just asking."

"You won't see any in the city except for the meat aisle at the grocery store. Bacon, roast, pork chops..."

"Tell me more about California."

Boss was not in the mood for small talk, but he spoke anyway. "California and Los Angeles, in particular, is a popular tourist state. People come from all over to visit the beaches, Hollywood, Disneyland. There are all kinds of attractions. It's a busy place."

"Why is Mames not with us? Why's she taking her own flight out?"

"I'm not sure," he answered. "I think Lara needs some alone time. You know, to sort things out, rest."

"I don't think so. I think you hurt her feelings."

Boss turned to her. "Now what would make you say that?"

"She was crying. She said she was tired, but that wasn't it. She was upset. What did you do?"

"Hey, now. I didn't do anything." He threw his hands in the air. He had done nothing but tell her he loved her. That was too much to put on Kamia. She loved Lara just as he did. "Sometimes, things are just not meant to be."

"Like you and me?"

"We're together now, right?"

"Yeah, but—" she hesitated. "All my life I dreamed of a father. Sometimes, in my dreams, he would come and save me from my life and then, in others, he was always there. And now that you are here, it seems so unreal."

"Did he look like me?"

"Nope."

"What'd he look like?"

"Tall, dark and handsome."

"Oh, then he did look like me."

Kamia laughed. "Keep dreaming."

They fell into a long silence before Kamia spoke again.

"Mames said she would teach me to read and write. That's still okay, right?"

Boss stared out the big picture window, not really seeing. How did he answer that question? Would Lara still want to teach her?

"I can get you any tutor you want. There are plenty of great tutors out there."

"I want Mames to teach me."

"Kamia, she's not qualified—"

"Fine. I'll be a mudoru the rest of my life."

Boss turned to her. "Kamia, you are not dumb or slow. You will do fine with any tutor who —"

"I want Mames," she repeated.

"How do you say hard-headed in your language?"

Kamia smiled. "Please? I like her, and she knows me. I'm shy around people I don't know."

"You don't seem too shy around me."

"Ugh. Mudoru, it is."

Boss chuckled. He loved the girl, attitude, and all. And he loved Lara. How would he be able to get her off his mind with her in the house teaching Kamia? "Fine. I have a deal for you."

"What?"

"When we get back, you can call her and make arrangements. At her house. I'll make sure you get there. That is, if she still wants to do it."

"She does." Kamia's face held a grin of satisfaction.

She'd won the battle but not the war. Boss was not one of those guys whose heart could be wrapped... Lara. She had his heart twisted and tied in knots. He remembered their kisses. So sweet and... sweet.

How would he ever get to sleep at night with her stuck in his head? His heart ached like never before. Except for Isa. And with Kamia, he held a part of Isa. It was more than he could ask for after all these years. He could no longer hold contempt for her. Only fond memories, and those of what could have been. But it wasn't in God's plan, and he was willing to accept that.

"Now boarding..." the call came, and he rose. Lara was nowhere in sight. She'd either taken another flight or was hiding — from him.

14

wo months later...

Kamia and Lara sat at the kitchen table getting ready for their lesson. It was unbelievable how much the girl had learned in such a short time. Highly intelligent, Kamia had caught on to the basics of reading and writing much quicker than Lara had thought. She'd zipped through a stack of childhood readers and had graduated to the smaller chapter books in no time. She thought them corny and immature, but she could read them.

"We have a new place," Kamia said. "Boss says I won't have to sleep on the pull-out couch in the living room anymore."

"Oh. That's great. How's your dad doing?"

Lara twirled the twine ring she still held on her finger. Her promise ring. Even after two months, she couldn't bring herself to take it off. It was a reminder of what she almost had. She tried not to ask about Boss too often. She was the one who had blown *him* off this time, and it wasn't fair to keep pining over what could have been.

"He's okay, I guess. He misses you."

"Why do you say that?"

"He pretends he's happy, but he's not."

"I don't know what to do about that. I mean, it's probably too late."

"No way. You can't use that one. I met him after years of not knowing him at all. I admit, at first, I wanted nothing to do with him, but now I'm glad I did. And I'm not just saying that because he bought me this cool cell phone. He's a good guy, Mames. He loves you."

Mames. She loved that the girl still used the endearment. She loved Kamia and not seeing Boss was tearing her to pieces.

"What do I do?" There she was again, taking advice from a teenager.

"Go see him. Call him. Send him a text. Anything."

"Maybe I could. I mean, a text. If he doesn't answer—"

"He will answer."

"You think so?"

"Bet." Kamia held out her hand to shake.

Lara pushed it away. "Since when do you bet?"

"Since now. Do it. I dare you."

"What do I say?"

"You know. Say something like 'I miss you, let's talk' or, I know, how about, 'you are so hot. I want to date you', something like that."

The wonderful world of teens. It transcended all nationalities. "I'll think about it. Come on, let's get some work done."

Kamia opened her book. "Promise me you will. You two are worse than him and my mother. She loved him too, but she was too proud, and she lost him. We lost him." Kamia gave her a pleading look. "Don't lose him."

"Yeah, okay. I'll do it. But let's get this work done, okay?"

"Okay." Kamia raised her brow. "Just don't chicken out."

After another hour of tutoring Kamia, her father sent a driver to pick her up. Lara sat on her couch and thought about what the girl had said. Could she text him? On the surface, it seemed like a great idea. If he didn't return it, then she would know, and if he did, well, that would be even better. But what would she say?

Her phone rang. It was Chloe.

"Hey, how are you doing?" Lara asked.

"I haven't slept a wink since this baby was born. How are you doing? Captured any bongo pigs lately?"

"That's boonie pigs, and that would be a no. How's the baby?"

"She's so cute! I don't know when I have ever been so blessed."

"Hey what about me?" Max called in the background.

"Yes, you too, honey. You have blessed my life like no other."

Lara laughed. "Gotta be sure he gets his lovin' on."

"Yes. He's been a great help, though. We take turns getting up with the baby. He helps feed her and has even changed a couple of diapers."

"I'm so happy for you."

"Then why don't you sound happy? You haven't been by to see her in almost a month. What happened, Lar?"

She hadn't been by to see the baby because she knew the moment Chloe saw her, she'd know something was wrong. She'd tried her best to hide it the last time, but it was too hard. They'd been friends since high school. Not much got past Chloe.

"It's Boss, isn't it? Something happened on that island. Why won't you talk about it?"

"It's stupid, really. He did nothing but profess his love for me." A tear slid down her face. "And I brushed him off like it was nothing. I told him... I'm so stupid."

"What did you tell him? I know you care for him."

"I said I didn't have time for... I am so... What do I do, Chloe? It's breaking my heart. I can't think. I can't eat. I'm a mess."

"You need to tell him how you feel. Boss cares for you. I know he does."

"How do you know?"

"He told you, didn't he? Boss isn't one to mince words."

"Yeah, he did. But it's too late. He hasn't called. He won't even drop Kamia off. He sends someone else to bring her. I blew it, Choe."

"If he cares for you, he'll forgive you. Just call him."

"But what if—"

"People don't stop loving each other over a quarrel. He loves you. You love him. I don't see the problem."

I'm the problem. "How? I don't even know his new address. They're moving into a bigger house for Kamia."

"If you want the address, I can get it for you."

There was no way she would show up on his doorstep. No way. "Kamia suggested I text him."

"That's a great idea. And if he doesn't respond, well, that's the end of it. But he will. I know Boss. He's had it rough, but he will respond."

Goosebumps lined Lara's arm, and the knot in her stomach tightened. Maybe she didn't want to know. Maybe it was better not knowing. "I'm scared."

"You want me to call him? You know I will. Better yet, I'll have Max go over there and—"

"No!" Lara yelled. "Chloe, please don't call him."

"Then you'll text him?"

"Yes. I'll text him. Just don't call him. I don't want him to think I'm a big baby who can't handle her own business."

"Okay, then. I'll stay out of it as long as you promise."

"I promise." The thought scared her half out of her mind, but what did she have to lose? She was already miserable and alone. Even the thought of buying a cat didn't appeal to her.

Lara hung up the phone and scrolled through her contacts. She found his name and pushed the button. Her finger hovered over the text button. What would she say? She pushed the button and stared at the open text.

Not knowing just what to write, she allowed her hands to do the talking. *Meet me tomorrow for a cup of coffee? Coco's 9 am. My treat.*

Before she could back out, she hit send. Wanting to take it back, she stared at her phone, waiting for a response. Nothing. She put the phone down and got into the shower. Don't think about it.

The day passed, and Lara went to her phone a thousand times. Still no answer. Her heart hurt from the dismissal, but somehow, she kept moving. Putting on her favorite movie, Sweet Home Alabama, she sat on the couch and watched. The happy ending she remembered by heart would cheer her up.

❦

Moving to a new place was a horrendous effort. How was Boss to know that he'd have to schedule a mover a week in advance? Every single place in town was booked, and he refused to let his daughter sleep on the pull-out couch one more night. He could have pulled some strings and had ten workers over there hauling his stuff away, but staying busy was the key to keeping his mind off his troubles.

Chandler and Max were there to help him move. He'd rented the biggest U-Haul he could get on short notice and the three of them, along with supervisor Kamia, lifted and heaved all their furniture and belongings into the truck.

The day before, Kamia had picked out a new bedroom set, and it was due to be delivered to the house later that day. Her excitement over getting her own bedroom set warmed his heart. He'd learned the girl had never had her own bed.

"Stop clowning around with that!" he called to Max, who was trying to balance one of his glass cases on his head. "That model is a classic."

Max brought it down in front of him. "Sure, Cal. Just trying to have a little fun."

"Do it on your own time," he bellowed. "I don't pay you to break things."

"You don't pay me at all!" Max called out. "Speaking of, I want a raise."

"Great, I'll double your salary."

"Ah cool man, wait—" He chuckled. "Zero times zero is... I'll take it!"

"Y'all play too much," Chandler said. "Hey wanna hear the good news?"

"You bought a new plane?" Boss asked.

"Nope, not yet. That's still pending investigation."

"Wait, wait, I got it. You finally broke down and hired a new assistant."

"What? And replace you? Nothing doing my man."

"Oh, I was just an assistant? Is that how you see me, bro?"

"Uh, no man. We were... Dena's pregnant!"

"Again?" Max asked. "Where you gonna put all these rug-rats?"

Boss sat on the floor between boxes and listened to them ramble. He wasn't in the mood for their back-and-forth jibes.

"You better watch it dude, or I'll tell Chloe you called yours a tax-deduction the other day!"

"Don't you go ratting me out, man," Max said. "I love my little tax-deduction."

Boss reached into his pocket to check the time, but it came up empty. "Hey, where's my phone? Kamia!" He stood.

Kamia came into the living room holding a stack of clothes. "I'm trying to get my stuff packed. What's up?"

"My phone. You didn't pack it, did you?"

"I didn't touch your phone. By the way, did you get any interesting texts recently?"

Boss looked at Max and then Chandler. "What's she talking about?"

"She's your tax-deduction," Max answered. "Not mine."

"His what?" Kamia asked, and the three of them laughed. "Whatever. You guys are weird." Kamia made her way back into the bedroom.

It wasn't often that Boss understood the girl. He and teenage girls were like water and oil. But they got along pretty well.

"It's probably in a box somewhere," he said. "Let's get this stuff loaded. I want to be in my house by the end of the night."

"You got it, Boss." Chandler saluted him.

"Aye aye, captain." Max picked up a box and headed for the door.

They were clowns, but they were the best he had, and he was thankful for them. Both had wives and families waiting for them at home, and they'd taken the time to come out and help him. He was grateful.

Boss grabbed a box and headed to the truck. It would be a long night, for sure. Maybe only one more trip before everything was at his new two-story, thirty-four hundred square foot home. Still small by billionaire standards, but Boss didn't believe a man was made by the size of his house or his bank account.

Sitting on the front step, box and all, Boss thought about Lara. For the millionth time, he tried to figure out what he'd done wrong. How he'd pushed her away. Maybe he should call her. Explain to her again how he felt. Beg her to believe him. At the moment, that was off the table. He had no idea where his phone was. Even if he did, he doubted he'd have the courage to call. He'd done the same with Isa. He could have gone back to see her. Beg her to reconsider. If he had, maybe he'd have known she was carrying his child. But he didn't. It was nothing but sheer pride. *Pride cometh before the fall...* Didn't he know that verse well? He'd lived it.

"What's up, buddy?" Max sat next to him.

"Who knew I had this much stuff? I'm beat." He played it off.

"That's it?"

"Yup. That's it. Just tired."

"Okay, man." Max patted him on the back. "If you say so. But I have it on good authority that some young lady had the hots for you." Max stood and made his way into the condo.

"Wait." Boss jumped up and followed him. "Who? Where did you hear that?"

"Mum's the word. Promised the wifey."

"Tell me, man," Boss said.

"You don't know, I ain't telling. No way I'm getting in the doghouse with Chloe."

Max didn't need to say anymore. Chloe and Lara were best friends. He was talking about Lara. She cared. "Bet whoever it is, is really beat up about it." He fished for more.

"Hah!" Max grabbed a box and headed out the door. He wasn't biting.

Suddenly he had the urge to call her. Beg her to hear him out. "Where's my phone!" he called again, but no one answered. "Ugh." He'd have to search through every box in the place once he got it all unloaded. Tomorrow. He would call her tomorrow. And he would beg her to reconsider. Get on his knees if he had to.

15

*L*ara sat at Coco's waiting. He hadn't answered her, but still, she came in hopes he would show. Maybe something had happened? He hadn't even answered to tell her he wasn't interested.

An older couple sat at a table across from her. They had to be in their seventies. The balding man was all decked out in dress pants with a button-down shirt. Suspenders held up his pants. Bright red socks peeked out from underneath. The woman was gray-haired and wore a floral muumuu that stopped at her knees. Holding hands across the table, they made idle chat. Lara wanted that kind of love. To grow old with someone, be gray-haired and still look across the table and be totally and completely enamored with that person. And she wanted it to be Boss.

She glanced at the clock on the wall behind her. It was nine forty-five. Boss wasn't going to show. He had moved on. He and his daughter. She had nothing left.

The door opened, and Lara looked up in anticipation for the thousandth time since she'd got there. Another sweet couple wandered in, holding hands. This time they were younger. Only a bit older than her. She took in a deep breath, trying not to cry.

The couple took a seat in the corner, and the barista rushed over to take their order. Coco's was a favorite in town. The coffees were expensive, but the taste was beyond compare.

Lara looked at the clock again. Only three minutes had passed. She stared out the window at the cars rushing by. They were all in such a hurry. A group of people ran across the street, laughing and carrying on. Lara couldn't place the emotions she got since coming back to civilization. Did any of those people get how easy their lives were? Had she become cynical? Maybe a little, but mostly she was grateful. God had shown her just how easy her life was and now she couldn't figure out why all the strangers around her didn't know how, at any moment, their lives could flip upside down, and they would have to rely on God completely and fully to survive. Of course, they didn't. Never had they been tasked with gutting a pig to stay alive.

The world was a different place to her now. Her parents had taught her God's grace and forgiveness, but she'd never fully understood it until God spoke to her under the water that day. As she struggled to get her life preserver unstuck from that faulty airplane, He had assured her she would survive. Only moments later she'd gotten the preserver unlatched and floated to the top. He had been right then, and He was still right now. With or without Callan Hemsworth, she would survive. With new courage to face the world, Lara stood. She would not allow pain to rule her life any longer.

The door opened again, and a man came rushing through. Her heart stopped. With an empty coffee cup in one hand and a half-eaten bagel in the other, she sat back down. Her heart beat like a drum in her chest. It was the man she'd been waiting for. He wore a pair of wrinkled jeans with a dirty t-shirt half tucked in. The rest flopped down over his pants. His hair was disheveled, and he looked like he'd just rolled out of bed. Looking around the room, his gaze caught hers. In an instant he was there, standing in front of her. He held her eyes as he stared deeply into them. Fear wafted over her as if her plane was going down once again. Why did he come? He hadn't answered her text. How did he know she would be here waiting for him to show?

"I'm sorry." He sat down across from her and held her eyes with his.

She twisted her twine ring nervously around her finger. He looked down at her hand and smiled.

"You still have it on."

She nodded. "You didn't answer. I thought you wouldn't come." Her voice sounded strange to her. Weak.

"I just found my phone. We were moving, and it was... I found it at the bottom of a box." He raked a hand through his hair. "As soon as I saw your text, I prayed I wouldn't miss you."

Lara smiled. It was so good to see him. "Thanks for coming." *Don't get your hopes up. So he came. That doesn't mean a thing.*

"You said you were buying me coffee?" He gave her that handsome smile she fell in love with.

"Sure. What would you like?"

"Whatever... a... I just wanted to see you. I missed you."

Her heart soared out of her chest and through the roof. "You did?"

"You didn't miss me?"

She raised her brows. Her mother's voice rolled through her head. *If you play hard to get, you won't get got.* "I did."

The barista rushed over to take his order. "What'll you have?"

"Whatever she's having." He looked down at her caramel latte and changed his mind. "Uh, just a coffee, black."

"Muffin, Bagel?"

"Yeah, sure."

Lara covered a giggle. It was good to see him nervous. "I think that was a multiple-choice question."

"It was? Oh. No, thank you."

The barista wrinkled her nose at him and walked away. Before Lara could say anything, he spoke. "I am so sorry."

"You said that. But I am not sure why you are sorry. I'm the one who pushed you away."

He gazed at her. "Lara, I am sorry." He said for the third time. "I didn't get why you were so angry with me. I mean, I was telling you how I felt, and you didn't believe me. At first, I was mad. I mean, we

154

shared so much on that island. We kissed, and I thought you felt the same way I did. But then I got it."

The barista set his coffee on the table. He pushed it aside and proceeded as if the woman was not there. "I pushed you away at the beginning, after that first date. I was stupid. It was my stupid pride, arrogance, fear. Give it whatever name you want, but I love you. From the day I met you, I've loved you."

"I love you, too." It was out before she could grab ahold of it.

"I mean—" He stopped. "You do?"

"I'm sorry, too." Lara could take it no longer. She loved him, and she understood why he pushed her away in the beginning. "You were trying to tell me back on the island, but all I could think about was that you were lonely and not thinking right. It was like we were the last two people on the face of the earth." She pulled at her ring. "I told you I didn't want a relationship because I was scared. I wanted to apologize, but then that helicopter came, and I knew I wouldn't be the only one anymore. I thought you would go back to your life and forget about me."

"I didn't. You are all I have thought about for every second of every minute of every — well you understand. I've been miserable. Kamia tells me I look like a lost boonie pig."

Lara smiled. It sounded just like Kamia. "I want to be sure I am the only one for you. I can't take another—"

"You are the one, Lara. The only one. I want to spend the rest of eternity with you. I want to get married and grow old with you. Have babies and laugh and smile. With you."

"I want that, too. All of it."

"You are my one and only." He raised his hands high, making the older couple look their way. "On the face of God's green earth. You are the only one for me."

The couple clapped, and Lara's face heated. "Shhh," she said.

"No. I'm not going to shush. I've been quiet too long. I've lived my life trying to avoid love, trying to get over old hurts or bury myself in them. I don't know, but I do know this. Lara, I love you."

"Ask her, boy. Now's your chance," the old man called.

Boss reached over and slid the twine ring from her finger and held it up to her.

"Lara Davies," he said. "Wait, do you have a middle name?"

Lara trembled at the thought of what he was about to do. "Ann" she squeaked out.

Boss slid from the chair and got on one knee. "Lara Ann Davies, you are the only woman on the face of this earth for me. I don't have a ring yet, but if this one will do until we can buy another, I will happily buy you the biggest, shiniest diamond ever made, if you'll only say you'll marry me."

The knot that had been tied so tight in her stomach broke free as love once again took over. Boss stared at her, waiting for her answer.

"What's it going to be, little lady?" the man called. "We having a wedding or not?"

Lara looked down at the ring that meant so much to her. It was a promise ring, and now an engagement ring. She loved it more than any diamond he could buy her.

"Yes!" Lara answered. By that time, tears streamed down her cheek, tears of pure unadulterated happiness.

Boss pulled out his wallet, threw a twenty on the table, then picked Lara up, and held her in his arms. "I will be the best husband, ever. I promise." He kissed her, and the handful of people in the coffee shop stood and clapped.

Boss carried her out of the shop and dropped her gently into the front seat of his new SUV. He rushed to the driver's side and slid in. He leaned in and kissed her again.

"Should we tell Kamia the good news?" he asked.

"Sure. That would be great."

"Good, because I have to go home and shower and change. I threw these on, hoping I wouldn't miss you."

"I can tell." She leaned in and kissed him again. She would never get tired of kissing him. Not ever.

As they walked in the door of his new home, Boss couldn't help but imagine it with Lara in it. Sharing his kitchen, sitting on his couch, sleeping in his bed. Being close to her was all he wanted.

"Kamia!" He yelled.

"Yeah?" she called back.

"I need to teach that child some manners," he said with a chuckle. "Come down here a minute. I have something to tell you."

Thumping down the stairs, Kamia reached the bottom and slid across the hardwood floors, almost breaking her neck. She righted herself and stood.

"Yeah?" As soon as she saw Lara, her lips widened into a huge smile. "You did it? You texted him?"

Lara nodded.

He didn't ask. He didn't want to know. Whatever Kamia and Lara had cooked up had worked, and he didn't care that they had cooked up this plan. He was happy about it.

"Have a seat. We want to talk to you."

"Whatever it is, I didn't do it. I've been up in my room putting clothes away." She held a hand up. "God's honest truth."

"He proposed!" Lara squealed. "We're getting married!"

"What!" Kamia squealed. "You proposed? You really did it?"

"Really did it," Boss answered. "Meet your new mommy." Boss chuckled at his own joke. Lara could never replace Isa in Kamia's life. Boss had finally learned to let go. Lara couldn't replace his first true love either. He wasn't looking for a replacement, he'd found a new love.

"I'm so excited. What did you say?" She bounced into the seat next to Lara, who sat with her on the couch in the middle of piles of stacked boxes. "I mean, obviously you said yes, but how'd you get through that hard head of his?"

"I am standing right here, you know." Boss put his hand on his hips.

Kamia stuck her tongue out and turned back to Lara. "We're going to be family! I'm so excited!"

"We are going shopping for a ring. Want to come?" Boss asked.

"Yes, of course, I do."

"Wait." Lara put her ringed hand up. "Boss, no."

"What?"

"I don't want an engagement ring. I want this one. It means so much to me. A promise ring, remember?"

Boss remembered. He'd promised never to hurt her again. And then he'd gone and broken it. "Are you sure? Lara that ring is made of —"

"Love. It's made of love."

"Okay. No ring. But when that one gets old and worn, we get you an official ring."

Lara nodded. "But it won't."

"Okay, then." Boss gave in.

If it meant that much to her, it was fine with him. "I'll let you two prattle on, while I get in the shower."

"When are you moving in?"

"Not until after the wedding."

"Right." Boss leaned over the back of the couch and kissed Lara. He winked at her, and she smiled.

As he headed to the downstairs shower, Lara and Kamia talked about wedding plans. Boss and Lara had agreed to wait a couple of months to be sure it was right. He didn't need to wait. It was right. He glanced back at her. Every thought was for her, every ounce of energy he had focused on the love of his life. The one he'd almost let get away. God had made a way for them, and he wasn't about to let pride or fear get in the way of his dreams. Not anymore. Closing the bathroom door, Boss undressed. He'd been so tired from moving the night before that he'd fallen into bed without searching for his phone or even taking a shower. He was sure he stunk of sweat.

"I want a sister," Kamia yelled from the living room. "Or a brother. A brother is good."

Boss chuckled. All his friends had babies, why not? He loved kids. And he'd missed so much of Kamia's upbringing. He was glad she was ready for a younger sibling because he was ready to make as many babies as Lara could manage.

"One's enough!" Lara called. "I mean, one more of course."

"Settle in," he called back. "I'm going for an even dozen."

The girls giggled. It was such a wonderful sound. As he turned on the shower, he couldn't stop the grin that filled his face. He was finally happy.

16

Hundreds of guests filled the wedding chapel. Lara's parents were so happy that she'd finally found the one. Her mother sat in the bride's room with her, her father just outside the door, waiting to walk her down the aisle.

Soon after the engagement, Lara had brought Boss home to meet them. They fell in love with him instantly. Full of nerves, she waited, her palms sweaty, for the wedding march to begin.

"You look lovely," Her mother said. "Don't be frightened."

"There're so many people out there. Even Grandma Edith came. I can't stop shaking."

"Oh, stop it. Grandma Edith loves you."

Grandma Edith was older than sin. And she was grumpy. Still, Lara managed to smile. "I bet she got us a cake decorating kit."

Her mother smiled.

Lara peeked out to see all her family and friends there, waiting for her to make her trek down the aisle. All three of her brothers sat together on the Bride's side. They'd all made it home to see their little sister finally tie the knot. A shock of disappointment hit her to see that Jewel was not there. She should have known. Although Lara had no way of contacting her sister, she'd hoped that somehow, she'd have gotten the word. She put the thought away. This was her day, and she wouldn't allow her younger sister to mess it up.

She rubbed her hands together. Her ring finger felt naked, but soon she would marry and would never depart from it again.

She was so nervous, she could hardly stand it.

"Close that door. What if he sees you?"

"He's seen me before, Mom. This isn't an arranged marriage."

"It's bad luck. Get back in here."

Lara took one last peek. Standing on the podium was her handsome husband with his best men, Chandler and Max. On the other side, waiting for her arrival, was her maid of honor, Kamia, and bride's maid Chloe. She mused about Chloe insisting Kamia be her maid of honor. She'd been so conflicted with wanting Kamia to have a special place in the wedding and having her best friend stand up for her. Chloe had insisted she choose Kamia. "She will soon be your daughter, after all." To Lara, Kamia was more than that. She was strong and brave, yet she had a heart of gold.

The music began.

"Are you ready?" her mother asked. "I'm going to go take my seat in the front."

"Yes." She squealed. "Thank you for staying back here with me." She hugged her mother and exited the bride's room.

Her father folded his arm around hers, and together they walked down the aisle.

"You look pretty as ever," he said, squeezing her arm.

Lara nodded, but her insides shook with fear. With each step, her body trembled.

"It's okay, honey. Focus on something else besides the crowd," her father said. "You'll do just fine."

So she did. The bridesmaids looked perfectly beautiful in their burgundy dresses and matching shoes. Their hair was all done up with flowers and vines. She looked at the crowd of people standing and smiling at her, and another nerve-wracking chill rushed through her body. *Focus on something else.*

The men stood so handsome in their black tuxes. Max grinned

that cheesy grin at her as the audience ogled her. *Focus on something else.* She made her way down the aisle, hoping she didn't trip on her long white lace gown. The same one her mother wore. Boss stared at her with such love in his eyes she thought she might faint. She broke the stare. She would have forever to look in those beautiful blues.

Out of the corner of her eye, she caught Chelsea. Standing next to her was a handsome man wearing a black suit. Zach. She'd heard so much about him. The man that turned Chelsea's life around. And the cute little girl between them stood on a chair to get a better view. Her arm draped comfortably over Chelsea's shoulders. Ana. Lara smiled and gave a small wave to them as she went by. It was not just a wedding, but a family reunion. The entire gang was there. All their broken hearts mended. Each of them whole and in love. But this was about her and Boss. And Kamia.

Lifting her dress, she stepped up to the podium and faced her soon-to-be husband. Standing next to Kamia and facing her husband, a tear fell down her cheek.

"I love you, Mames," Kamia whispered in her ear.

"I love you too, Kamia." She grabbed onto the girl's hand and held it, only letting it go when Boss was to put the gold-plated twine ring around her finger. Just as she said, it would last forever.

The crowd cheered as the newlyweds kissed, but it all sounded like a background noise shut out by the beating of her heart. She had found her happy ending.

ENJOYED THIS BOOK? YOU CAN MAKE A DIFFERENCE.

Do reviews intimidate you? Don't know exactly what to say? There is no right or wrong. As a reader, you have amazing influential power in helping others decide which books to read. If you enjoyed my words … please take a minute to write a few of your own and let others know.

To leave a review of – *Her Billionaire Chauffeur* –click here[1]

Thank you very much!

---

1. www.amazon.com/dp/b07k3659W3

SNEAK PEEK - HER BILLIONAIRE SCOUNDREL

CHAPTER 1

*J*ewel Davies stood on the doorstep of her sister's home, but didn't knock. Her clothes were wrinkled and soiled, and she'd lost so much weight they were nearly falling off. She hadn't brushed her hair in days, and she reeked of body odor. The last thing she wanted was for her sister to see her in her current condition, but there was nothing she could do about it. She didn't have a dime to her name to clean herself up, and the gas station bathroom was dirtier than she was.

Jewel ran a finger through her tangled hair, trying her best to smooth it out at least a little. What would Lara say when she saw her ragged condition? Her sister's pity was the last thing she wanted.

Staring down at her clothes she asked — *then why are you here?* She didn't know the answer to that question. *Look at yourself. How can anyone do anything but pity you? You're a mess. No one can ever love you if you don't love yourself.*

The words were true, and they came from her own heart, but Jewel was tired of running, screwing up her life, and being afraid. She wanted to make a change, and Lara was the only one who would look past her condition to see her intention.

Jewel sighed and gave the door a few small taps. Her emotions were a jumbled mix between wanting to see her older sister and turning away in a sprint. Neither was a choice she wanted to deal with, but she desperately needed help. Knocking again, louder this time, she shifted on her feet and ran her fingers through her knotted hair again.

Get over yourself, Jules. You made your bed.

Bulky footsteps sounded from the other side of the door, and only moments later, it opened. A tall, handsome man wearing a Raiders football jersey and blue jeans stood before her. He didn't speak. Instead, he stared at her as if she looked familiar and then again, altogether not. His face cocked sideways like an oversized Doberman, which proved his state of utter confusion. Sniffing the air, he wrinkled his nose.

Yep, I smell pretty bad.

Jewel stepped back, hoping to clear the air for him. Insecurity rushed through her in a wave of goosebumps.

I shouldn't have come.

Maybe the gas station bathroom wasn't such a bad idea after all. At least she could have cleaned up a little before making her appearance, but she had no idea anyone would be there but Lara. Shouldn't the billionaire be stuck in an office somewhere pouring over his work?

"Uh, hi. Can I help you?" The man glanced behind him into the house and then back to Jewel.

"I... uh, is Lara around?"

"Who is it, Boss?" a voice called from inside.

The mere sound of it incapacitated her. Her legs wobbled, and she was barely able to keep herself from falling to the ground.

No. I can't face her.

As her flight response kicked in, Jewel turned to run. She stepped off the porch, and her head spun. Her body trembled so erratically, she nearly lost her balance. In the background of her fuzzy brain, Lara's voice rang through from behind, and she slowed her pace.

"Jewel? Is that you?"

Jewel stopped in her tracks.

She couldn't meet her sister face to face. Why she thought she could was beyond her. Jewel continued her wobbly stride toward the broken-down car their older brother, Thomas, had given her only days before.

"Just get your life together, Jules," he'd said, handing her the keys. *"Mom and Dad can't take any more drama."*

The story of my life.

"Jewel, wait." A gentle hand touched her shoulder.

Tears flooded her face as she turned to see her sister for the first time in... way too long.

"I can't. It was a mistake coming here. I'm sorry."

"No, Jewel." Her sister's warm hand stayed on her shoulder. "Please. I want you to stay. At least come in for some tea. I have peach. Your favorite." Lara's eyes pleaded with her not to leave, and everything inside her told her to listen, but she was not brave. She was a coward.

"I have to... I should go."

Her sister begged her with those same eyes she'd given her the day she'd walked out the door of her family's home. She hadn't listened then. How dare she knock on her sister's door now, give her false hope, and then break her heart again? What kind of cruel-hearted person did that to her own sister?

You need her. If you really want to turn your life around. You have to stay. Try.

She was so tired of running. "Okay," she whispered in defeat. "Only for a minute, though."

Jewel scanned the area. She saw no suspicious vehicles. No one's watching eyes. How could she be sure she was not putting Lara in danger?

Following her sister into the house, Jewel noticed Lara's small protruding belly. She was pregnant. Her defenses kicked up another notch. She couldn't bring Lara and her family into her mess of a life. Especially not with a baby on the way. She'd done some bad things and was wanted by a guy who would do anything to get her back. And when he did, he would not be generous with her. She would stay for only a minute, and then she'd leave and never return.

"Have a seat, Jules. I'm so glad you came." Lara smiled, not saying a word about Jewel's obvious lack of hygiene.

Jewel stared at the man who watched her quietly. His face was blank, showing no sign of emotion one way or the other. Jewel had heard all about the rich tycoon Lara had met and married. Her first instinct when Thomas told her about it had been to try and get some money out of them, but seeing them now, she changed her mind. She'd vowed to put that life away, and she planned to stick to it if it killed her.

It just might.

If Liam found her, she'd be lucky to survive.

The memory of his words rolled through her head. *People don't just change, Jewel. You are what you are.* But Jewel didn't want that life anymore. She had to do whatever she could to get away from it. No matter what, she had to try.

Jewel sat down at the kitchen table across from Lara. Taking in her surroundings, she wondered if Thomas had exaggerated a bit in his evaluation of the man's financial situation. The house was nice, but certainly not billionaire-ish.

"Jewel, this is Boss. My husband."

Jewel nodded to the man and turned back to Lara. Her throat was parched and her lips chapped. "Maybe, I will have that tea." She had no idea when she had last eaten or had anything to drink.

Lara rose slowly as if she thought Jewel might run if she left the room. That evaluation was not too far off. Jewel was doing everything she could to not jump from her seat and sprint from the place. The only thing keeping her glued to her chair was that she missed her sister. Even if it were only for a moment, she would bask in the time she had with her. Once she left, she would stay gone. It was too dangerous to return.

"Yeah, sure. I'll grab some tea. Boss, why don't you have a seat. Chat with Jewel."

Boss took the seat next to her. "So, what brings you here?" His voice sounded cordial, yet guarded. She didn't blame him. She looked like a stray dog who had been kicked around one too many times. And that was precisely how she felt.

What had Lara told him about her? Whatever it was, it was probably not good, yet most likely true. "I uh, just popped in to say hi." *And possibly grab a nice, hot shower.* "I won't be long."

A teenage girl with warm dark skin bounced into the room. "Who's this?"

Jewel looked from Boss to the girl and then back again. The resemblance was subtle, but Jewel couldn't figure out the connection.

"Oh, hey, Kamia." Boss waved the girl over; seemingly happy he didn't have to be alone with her. "This is Lara's younger sister, Jewel."

"Are you guys twins?" Kamia stared at her and then yelled, "Mames! Why didn't you tell me you had a —" Her voice grew quiet as recognition kicked in. "Oh, right? The younger uh... sister. Good to meet you." Kamia drew closer, taking in her rancid odor. Her nose twitched a bit, but she played it off well.

Don't worry, girl, I am completely aware of my stench.

Jewel held in a grimace at the girl's cut off words. Did everyone in the family know about her wayward past?

"Uh, nice to meet you, Kamia." Still, she couldn't figure out the connection between the three of them.

As if reading her thoughts, Kamia said, "I'm Boss's daughter. We just met last year."

"Oh?" As if that made everything clear. Why hadn't Thomas told her about the girl? "It's good to meet you," she said again, for lack of something better to say.

"It's a long story," Boss said, seeing the confusion in her face. "Kamia lived in Guam before her mother passed away. I didn't know about her until it happened."

At that moment Lara came back into the room with a tray containing a pitcher of tea and a package of Oreos. Lara hadn't forgotten her favorite cookie. She set the tray on the table and sat across from Jewel. Her stomach gnawed at her for sustenance.

"Oh, hey, Kamia. I hope you don't mind. I'll get you a new pack."

"Yeah. It's cool," Kamia said. "I'd love to stay for this uh... family reunion, but I better get to my online classes. Math sucks by the way."

Kamia bounced back out of the room, as fast as she'd come, leaving the three of them to stare at each other uncomfortably. The silence was intolerable, and for the millionth time since she'd entered the home, Jewel was tempted to jump up and run.

Boss broke the silence. "It's good to have you here, Jewel. You're welcome to stay."

He pushed the cookies toward her. Saliva filled her mouth as her stomach begged her to eat. It took everything she had to not grab for them and devour the entire package in one bite.

Looking back at Boss, comprehension hit her. *Stay? In your home? I think not.*

Sleeping in her car was not the ideal situation, but the more she saw of her sister's family, the more she knew she couldn't stay with them. But she'd gladly take the cookies with her. Maybe even a quick shower. Jewel scratched at her dry skin. A bottle of lotion?

When she didn't answer, Lara spoke. "So, what brings you here?"

Boss stood. "I think I'll let the two of you talk. I've got some errands to run, anyway."

Lara nodded, and Boss leaned in and kissed her forehead. "I'll be back in a bit."

The room was silent until the sound of the garage door closed and then Lara spoke. "What's going on, Jewel? I haven't seen you in years. And you look like... a homeless person."

Jewel stared at the cookies and could take it no longer. She opened the package, grabbed greedily for a cookie, and popped one in her mouth. Washing it down with the peach tea, she contemplated her response.

"I, well, I just wanted to tell you how sorry I am for not making it to your wedding. And to say hi. I see you are preg —"

"Don't give me that, Jewel. You want something. What is it?"

"Why... I just..." Her past came crashing down on her. She was a horrible sister and an even worse human being. "You're right. I shouldn't have come." Jewel stood. "I'll be going now."

"Wait." Lara stood and extended a hand. "Let's just talk. I'm sorry. I shouldn't have been so harsh."

Jewel held her stance. "No. You were right. I have no excuse for... I shouldn't be here."

"Please, Jules. Stay. Let's get you cleaned up. I'll brush your hair like I did when we were kids."

At the sound of her familiar nickname, Jewel sunk back into her chair. She nodded but turned away from her sister. Before she could stop it, a rush of tears fled from her eyes like a tidal wave. Placing her head in her hands, she sobbed. Arms came around her, and she cried all the tears she'd held in for the last fifteen years. How could she do this to her sister? Her family?

"I'm sorry, Lara. I didn't know where else to go."

"What happened?" Lara rubbed her back. "Where have you been?"

Jewel took a deep breath and looked at her sister. There was no way she could tell her all the crazy events of the past fifteen years. She settled for giving her a half-truth. "I got into some trouble with the law, and I have kinda been on the run. But that's all cleared up now. My probation has ended, and I'm trying to turn my life around." Who was she kidding? Liam would never let that happen. Not in a million years.

"Do you have a job? A home? Where are you staying?"

Wasn't it obvious she had no home? No job.

Look at me. Who would hire a person looking like this?

Taking a deep breath, she pushed back the anger. All she needed was a little help up. A job. A place to lay her head. A shower. But she'd burned every bridge she'd ever created. Even her friends had stopped speaking to her.

"I'm staying in my car. I've been applying for jobs, but no one wants to hire a homeless person. I haven't even showered in ... this is too much. I should go."

"No, Jules." Lara placed a hand on hers. "Please stay. We have an extra room. I can help you get back on your feet. Please, I want to help."

She couldn't stay. It was too dangerous. Liam would find her. And if he did, it would not be good for anyone. She grabbed two more cookies and shoved one in her mouth.

"Please." Lara's eyes pleaded with her. "Just a month. We'll try it out for at least that long."

How could she tell her sister no? It was a chance of a lifetime. An opportunity to get her life back together. The only chance she had. It had been why she came in the first place.

The probability of Liam finding her there amongst the rich and worriless, was a far reach. She'd been able to evade him for months living on the streets. This area, it was one place he would never look. Not in a million years. Her confidence built a little, and she looked at her sister.

"Are you sure?"

"Please. Jewel, I want to help. If you leave now, I fear I'll never see you again."

The reality of it was much worse than Lara could ever imagine. It was what brought Jewel there in the first place. All she needed was a chance to start again.

"Okay," she whispered. "But only for a month."

Lara smiled. "It'll be okay, Jules. I promise."

Jewel wasn't so sure, but if she stayed out of the public eye, chances were, Liam wouldn't find her. He knew nothing about her family and would never suspect she had a sister on the wealthy side of town. Maybe it could work.

Full of hope, Jewel grabbed a few more cookies and ate greedily.

"Let me get you something more... uh, no offense, but why don't you jump in the shower and I'll make you something healthier than cookies."

"Yeah. None taken. I know I smell like a dead skunk."

Lara giggled. "Maybe not that bad. Nothing a nice hot shower won't cure."

"Oh, it's bad."

"Right this way." Lara stood. "I'll grab some clean clothes you can put on when you get out."

Jewel's nerves were already calming. A hot shower wouldn't fix all of her issues, but at least she'd be clean. A person could conquer the world if they had on a fresh pair of underwear.

Jewel followed Lara into the downstairs bathroom and turned on the shower while Lara left to grab her some clean clothes. A small amount of peace settled within her, and she was glad she came. It could work. It had to.

❧

Jackson Palmer paced his small apartment, clenching his hands in frustration. It had been two weeks since his mother passed, and he'd still not gotten what he'd been promised — the name of his father. For his entire life, his mother had been secretive about who the man was. Finally, on her deathbed, she'd promised the man's name would be revealed in her will.

His phone rang.

About time. "Yeah?" he answered.

"Jackson, this is Bartholomew, your mother's lawyer. I expected you here ten minutes ago. Where are you?"

"What? You said you were coming here."

"I don't make house calls, young man. If you want your mother's will read, I expect you to be here in five minutes."

"No way, man. You said you would be here. I've been waiting for you. Besides, I'm outta gas."

"Fine. I'm on my way out now. I'll be there in a few minutes." The phone clicked before Jax could respond.

"Good. You old geezer. Serves you right."

Jax rubbed his hands together. Finally, he would find out who his father was and take what was rightfully his.

The man was rich, that much Jax was sure of. Other than that, he was clueless to who he was or why the deadbeat hadn't helped his mother and him since Jax was born. Did he even know about him? Was he some secret love child?

Pacing once again, Jax couldn't tear his mind away from the news to come. He'd even endure the meeting with old Bart just to get his hands on the name of the dirty rat who knocked his mother up and then fled like a coward.

Ten minutes later the doorbell rang, and Jax headed straight for it. Running a hand over his scruffy chin, he slowed his pace. Did he really want to know who his father was? Would it do anything to change the miserable past he'd lived? Nope, but it sure could change the future. Yes, and that's what Jax was after. His father owed him big for leaving him out in the cold, and he would collect on every penny that was due to him.

Jax opened the door to the scrawny, weasel-looking man his mother had kept on to oversee her will. The guy was an ambulance chaser for sure. And those beady little eyes that stared out from behind his wire-framed glasses made him look like the rat he was.

"Well, if it ain't old Bart. 'Bout time you showed. Mom's been gone two whole weeks. You been spending her money on cheap Vodka and TV dinners?"

"May I come in? I want to make this quick. I have other, more important house calls to make."

The man never did like him. The feeling was mutual. "Thought you didn't make house calls."

The man cleared his throat. "May I come in or not?"

"Be my guest." Jax waved him inside. "Let's get down to business."

Bart made his way into the apartment. "Looks like your hoodlum activities are on the downside," he said, inspecting Jax's scantily furnished living room.

"What do you know about my activities? I'm in big business now. Got me a real job."

"From your undertakings in the past —"

"Look, man, I don't want you here anymore than you want to be. Let's get down to business."

Jax had always had a thing for numbers. He could con a cat out of a dollar by offering him two shiny quarters. And that accounting job he'd had, well, that only lasted a couple of months before the company found out he lied on his application. He'd saved them millions, but all they cared about was his "no" mark on the box asking if he'd had any prior felonies.

Bart wiped the couch cushion before sitting as if there might be contaminants that would soil his cheap, knock-off suit. Jax flopped down in the yard sale chair opposite him.

Bart snapped the buttons on his low-budget, fake-leather briefcase and pulled out a manila envelope. "Your mother, as you know, was completely broke when she passed. Her home was in a reverse-mortgage and has gone back to the bank. As we spoke of earlier, there are no monies to dispense."

"Yeah, once you got your filthy hands on it."

"I have charged her nothing but the standard rate." Bart pushed his glasses up on his nose. "Now, she did leave you the information you requested, and you will find it all right here." He pushed the envelope to Jax and stood. "I'll be going now."

Jax stared at the envelope. It was thin and sealed. Over the top was a layer of invisible tape. His hands burned to open it right there, but he preferred to be alone when he did. So, he stood and walked the old geezer to the door.

"Yeah, I'll see you out."

The man held out his hand to shake, and Jax passed him up, heading for the door.

"One more thing." Bart followed him.

"What? You want to wish me a Merry Christmas?"

"Ah, well, if you like, but actually, well, really, I guess it's a Christmas in July gift of sorts." The man snapped back open his case and handed another sheet of paper to Jax. Fishing in his shirt pocket for a pen, he handed it over.

"Yeah. Too bad it's only June. What's this?"

"It's a birth record."

"For who? What's this about?"

"It's for your brother."

"My what?"

"I did some digging around and found out a couple of things for you. Free of charge, of course. Not that you have appreciated my service to your mother. Nevertheless, you will understand when you open that." He nodded to the envelope in Jax's hand. "Good luck. I hope you find all you are looking for."

Without another word, the man opened the door and walked out, leaving Jax to stare at the two items in his hand. The guy had actually been somewhat kind to him, and that was disturbing. He watched the man saunter to his car and closed the door.

Heading back to the couch, Jax opened the birth certificate. *Chandler Jones.* The guy was born only five months earlier than he.

I have a brother.

His hand shook as he slid his finger under the flap of the envelope from his mother. Pulling out one handwritten sheet of paper, he opened it and read.

J ackson,

In life, sometimes people make mistakes they can never take back. I've made my fair share, but the affair I had with your father was something I never regretted. If I hadn't, that would mean I'd have never gotten pregnant with you. I could never regret that. The first time I saw your cute little face, I was consumed with uncontainable joy. That day, lying in the hospital, holding my sweet baby boy, I gave my life to Christ, and He forgave me of my sin. I hope you can forgive me, too.

I am genuinely sorry for all the years I have kept your father a secret. It was something I had to do. I did it for you. Your father was a very powerful man, and the knowledge of your birth would have sent all of our lives in a tailspin we could never come back from.

Now that I am gone, I feel it only right you should know where you came from. Your father, Clifton Jones, passed away some years back. I know this does no good to you now, but I hope the knowledge of it will give you some closure.

· · ·

J ackson dropped the paper to the floor.

He's dead? My father is dead?

All this time, he could have gone to the man and made him pay for leaving him and his mother to fend for themselves. And now the man was dead. Heatedly, Jackson snatched back up the page and continued to read.

I *love you, Jax. And I know somewhere deep down in that broken heart of yours you will find it in your heart to forgive me as well as your father. You are a smart man. You can be whatever you set your mind to. I'm asking that you put away your pride and set your heart to doing something better with your life. I'll be watching from above. Make me proud.*

Mom.

T ears flooded Jax's eyes. He'd given his mother such a rough time throughout his life, and still, she believed in him. If only he could believe in himself. But his father — Jax would never forgive him. Not ever. Dead or not, the man would forever taint his soul as black as soot.

He set the letter down and picked up the birth certificate again. He read the top line.

Chandler Jones.

Did he receive Daddy's fortune? Was he sitting up in some CEO's office, spending the money that rightfully belonged to him? At least half of it, anyway. This Chandler guy, he was the legitimate son. He bore his father's last name, but did that entitle him to the man's entire fortune?

Jax wiped his face on the sleeve of his shirt as a plan formed in his head. He would find the guy if it were the last thing he did, and he would demand his share. As sure as his mother was buried six-feet under in a cold grave, he would find him.

HAVE YOU READ THESE TITLES?

Beached with a Billionaire

Somer has made the worst mistake of her life. After losing everything, she moved across the country to start over. Her only goal is to get a job, pay the bills, and forget the awful past. When her last remaining friend convinces her to go on a single's cruise, it's the last thing she wants to do, but reluctantly she agrees.

Torn between the deception of his ex-wife, and the love for a son he thought was his. Benjamin is looking for some peace and quiet. A cruise to Jamaica might be just the thing, only he has no idea that his secretary has booked him on a single's cruise.

They meet, and the connection is undeniable, but neither of them are ready to deal with the pain of their pasts. Can a mishap in Jamaica be what they need to set their stranded hearts into a new direction?

The Cowboy's Forbidden Bride

After the loss of her parents, Charlotte struggles to keep the family ranch going for her and her younger brother, Cole.

Ezra has a criminal past he'd like to escape, so when his boss pushes him too far, he runs despite the consequences.

When Cole rides up with a dying stranger strapped to the back of his horse, Charlotte recognizes the man she's met only once but never forgot. He doesn't want to put her life in danger, but he's too weak to leave.

She knows she needs to send him away to protect Cole and the ranch, but she'll do anything she can to keep him there...

The Act of Falling

Bekah, a singer at a local Long Beach night club, is a magnet for bad boys. When her boyfriend, Blade, gets arrested, she leaves everything behind, including her beloved guitar, to find something ... else. Out of gas but with a plan, Bekah stops in the pristine little town of Sunshine, Arizona.

Ezekiel, the son of the town preacher, is also a teacher at the church's private school. He's quite content in his life and secure in his surroundings. Well, mostly ... From the moment Bekah shows up in the church office, wearing a skirt shorter than a man's imagination, a hoop nose ring, and a tattoo of a spider on her back, Ezekiel's quiet little world shifts into territories unknown.

But no worries ... she'll be gone by morning.

The Law of Falling

An officer of the law, a social worker, an ornery grandmother, and a flat tire.

When Samantha's grandmother takes a fall in her home, Samantha's parents worry she's not fit to live alone anymore. To her disdain, Samantha seems to have drawn the short straw and now must go out and evaluate her grandmother's situation.

It's only been a short time since Garrett has graduated from the police academy, and being a police officer is nothing like he'd thought. He is sorely missing the kids at the church where he used to teach. But when an attractive woman rolls into town with a flat tire, Garrett is intrigued with the newcomer.

Before they know it, Samantha and Garrett find themselves spending time together, and Gramma Matt may just be the cause of it...

The Billionaire's UnWelcome Home

A car crash reunited them, yet threatened to tear them apart.

After receiving word of his father's illness, Jesse James was hesitant to return home. He'd joined the military to get away from the billionaire and everything he stood for. But when his mother insisted he return, he conceded.

He was in no way prepared for what awaited him...

Monetarily, Maya's life couldn't be more perfect. Working for the James family, her son's every need was taken care of. That was, so long as she kept the family secret. But something was missing, and when Jesse showed up in town, Maya's life became much more complicated...

Love became a complication as Jesse and Maya fought for their right to become a family.

This is an interracial love story with racist themes.

Her Billionaire Dream

He's building an empire. She's cleaning it.

After years of reviving the family business from the ashes his father left, Chandler Jones has no time for a serious relationship. He has no need for companionship and only dates his high school sweetheart because she's equally rich, extremely independent, and looks good on his arm. But when she ducks out on him on the most important weekend of the year, Chandler is desperate.

Dena Gysler wants nothing to do with her rich, arrogant employer. She cleans his office, and he has no idea she exists which suits her just fine. When he offers her ten thousand dollars to accompany him to his weekend business conference, Dena is appalled. But ten thousand dollars is a lot of money for a cleaning lady to refuse.

Dena and Chandler agree to a strictly-business plan that will benefit them both. And falling in love is not a part of that plan.

But then again ... plans change.

To find out more about these characters and their lives check out the rest of the stories in this series.

Her Billionaire Jackpot — Max and Chloe — Mixed-up Marriage
Her Billionaire Wish — Zach and Chelsea — Cruise Ship Romance
Her Billionaire Chauffeur — Boss and Lara — Stranded Together
Her Billionaire Scoundrel — Jax and Jewel — Road Trip

Finding Alissa

When Alissa Martin finds out her fiancé is cheating on her, she's so distraught that she packs a suitcase and leaves. Too upset to think of anything but her fiancé's deception, she ends up in a car accident. Upon awakening in the hospital in the town of Trust, Arizona, she has lost her memory.

Already confused and frustrated, she is shocked when the stranger in her room tells her that she's a loving wife and mother of three.

Even after a year, Derek Andrews mourns the loss of his wife. But his wealthy father-in-law thinks it's time to move on. So much so, that he threatens to cut Derek off if he doesn't find a mother for the children. But could he ever love another woman?

When he comes upon the wreckage of a woman who looks identical to his Elle, he devises a scheme to make her a part of their family...

To find out more about these characters and their lives check out the rest of the stories in this series.

Loving Josie — A Rags to Riches Story
Reclaiming Bailey — A Second Chances Story
Chasing Kennedy — An Online Love Story

To read these and more click on Tayla Alexandra's Author Page to see her full list of books.

GET FREE BOOKS AND EXCLUSIVE TAYLA ALEXANDRA MATERIAL

Connecting with readers is one of the greatest things about writing. I send a weekly newsletter with details on new releases, special offers, and other news tidbits related to my writing.

By signing up for my mailing list, not only will you get exclusive insider news, I'll send you the following titles for free in your choice of Kindle, ePub, or pdf versions

To Trust Again, A Novella

Brother of the Bride, A novelette

Wrapped in Love, A Christmas short

Sign up here[1] for exclusive member access and your free ebooks.

---

1. https://storyoriginapp.com/giveaways/239786da-1dd4-11eb-abef-0b6dedf859eb

ABOUT THE AUTHOR

Tayla Alexandra is the author of Her Sweet Billionaire Romance Series, Finding Trust Romance Series among several others. She makes her online home at Tayla Alexandra Books. You can connect with Tayla on Twitter, on Facebook , and you can send an email at TAlexandraAuthor@gmail.com

f facebook.com/talexandraromance
y twitter.com/AlexandraTayla
a amazon.com/author/taylaalexandra
BB bookbub.com/profile/tayla-alexandra

Made in the USA
Columbia, SC
02 June 2025

58803105R00117